SPECIAL MESSAGE TO READERS

THE ULVERSCROFT FOUNDATION

PAW

re ... es.

Eye

eat

ınd

ɔgy,

up,

ərn

Please return on or before the latest date above.
You can renew online at *www.kent.gov.uk/libs*
or by telephone 08458 247 200

yal

Y ... on

I ... u

THE ULVERSCROFT FOUNDATION
The Green, Bradgate Road, Anstey
Leicester LE7 7FU, England
Tel: (0116) 236 4325

websit... roft.com

Charlotte Perkins Gilman was born in 1860 in Hartford, Connecticut; she was a writer and social activist during the late 1800s and early 1900s. Throughout her decade-long marriage to the artist Charles Stetson she suffered from severe depression and underwent a series of unusual treatments for it. This experience is believed to be the inspiration behind 'The Yellow Wall-Paper'. While best known for her fiction, Gilman was also a lecturer and intellectual, her most successful non-fiction work being *Women and Economics*, published in 1898, which called for women to become more economically independent. Along with writing books, Gilman also established *The Forerunner*, a magazine exploring women's issues and social reform. Published between 1909 and 1916, it featured essays, opinion pieces, fiction and poetry. She committed suicide in 1935 after being diagnosed with inoperable breast cancer. 'The Yellow Wall-Paper' remains Gilman's best-known work, a pioneering portrait of the trauma of depression that has lost nothing of its unsettling power.

THE YELLOW WALL-PAPER
AND OTHER STORIES

'The Yellow Wall-Paper' is Gilman's pioneering Gothic masterpiece, telling the story of a woman's descent into madness. Confined to a room, with only the intricate wallpaper for stimulation, the narrator slowly loses her grip on reality. She becomes increasingly suspicious of the people who care for her, convinced they are conspiring against her. As she becomes increasingly transfixed by the sprawling pattern on her walls, her horrifying fantasy becomes disturbingly real. Also contained in this collection are eighteen of her other stories, which exhibit her imaginative treatment of women removed from their traditional roles.

CHARLOTTE PERKINS GILMAN

THE YELLOW WALL-PAPER
AND OTHER STORIES

Complete and Unabridged

ULVERSCROFT
Leicester

The Yellow Wall-Paper; Circumstances Alter Cases; The Unexpected
First published in the United States of America in 1890

The Giant Wistaria; An Extinct Angel
First published in the United States of America in 1891

The Rocking-Chair; Through This
First published in the United States of America in 1893

Three Thanksgivings; According to Solomon
First published in the United States of America in 1909

The Widow's Might; The Jumping-Off Place; Turned; Making a Change
First published in the United States of America in 1911

A Council of War
First published in the United States of America in 1913

If I Were A Man; Mr Peeble's Heart
First published in the United States of America in 1914

Mrs Merrill's Duties; Girls and Land
First published in the United States of America in 1915

Joan's Defender
First published in the United States of America in 1916

This Large Print Edition
published 2015

The moral right of the author has been asserted

*A catalogue record for this book is available
from the British Library.*

ISBN 978–1–4448–2253–3

Published by
F. A. Thorpe (Publishing)
Anstey, Leicestershire

Set by Words & Graphics Ltd.
Anstey, Leicestershire
Printed and bound in Great Britain by
T. J. International Ltd., Padstow, Cornwall

This book is printed on acid-free paper

Contents

The Yellow Wall-paper

It is very seldom that mere ordinary people like John and myself secure ancestral halls for the summer.

A colonial mansion, a hereditary estate, I would say a haunted house, and reach the height of romantic felicity — but that would be asking too much of fate!

Still I will proudly declare that there is something queer about it.

Else, why should it be let so cheaply? And why have stood so long untenanted?

John laughs at me, of course, but one expects that in marriage.

John is practical in the extreme. He has no patience with faith, an intense horror of superstition, and he scoffs openly at any talk of things not to be felt and seen and put down in figures.

John is a physician, and *perhaps* — (I would not say it to a living soul, of course, but this is dead paper and a great relief to my mind —) *perhaps* that is one reason I do not get well faster.

You see he does not believe I am sick!

And what can one do?

If a physician of high standing, and one's own husband, assures friends and relatives that there is really nothing the matter with one but temporary nervous depression — a slight hysterical tendency — what is one to do?

My brother is also a physician, and also of high standing, and he says the same thing.

So I take phosphates or phosphites — whichever it is, and tonics, and journeys, and air, and exercise, and am absolutely forbidden to 'work' until I am well again.

Personally, I disagree with their ideas.

Personally, I believe that congenial work, with excitement and change, would do me good.

But what is one to do?

I did write for a while in spite of them; but it *does* exhaust me a good deal — having to be so sly about it, or else meet with heavy opposition.

I sometimes fancy that in my condition if I had less opposition and more society and stimulus — but John says the very worst thing I can do is to think about my condition, and I confess it always makes me feel bad.

So I will let it alone and talk about the house.

The most beautiful place! It is quite alone, standing well back from the road, quite three miles from the village. It makes me think of English places that you read about, for there are hedges and walls and gates that lock, and lots of separate little houses for the gardeners and people.

There is a *delicious* garden! I never saw such a garden — large and shady, full of box-bordered paths, and lined with long grape-covered arbors with seats under them.

There were greenhouses, too, but they are all broken now.

There was some legal trouble, I believe, something about the heirs and co-heirs; anyhow, the place has been empty for years.

That spoils my ghostliness, I am afraid, but I don't care — there is something strange about the house — I can feel it.

I even said so to John one moonlight evening, but he said what I felt was a *draught*, and shut the window.

I get unreasonably angry with John sometimes. I'm sure I never used to be so sensitive. I think it is due to this nervous condition.

But John says if I feel so, I shall neglect proper self-control; so I take pains to control myself — before him, at least, and that makes me very tired.

I don't like our room a bit. I wanted one downstairs that opened on the piazza and had roses all over the window, and such pretty old-fashioned chintz hangings! but John would not hear of it.

He said there was only one window and not room for two beds, and no near room for him if he took another.

He is very careful and loving, and hardly lets me stir without special direction.

I have a schedule prescription for each hour in the day; he takes all care from me, and so I feel basely ungrateful not to value it more.

He said we came here solely on my account, that I was to have perfect rest and all the air I could get. 'Your exercise depends on your strength, my dear,' said he, 'and your food somewhat on your appetite; but air you can absorb all the time.' So we took the nursery at the top of the house.

It is a big, airy room, the whole floor nearly, with windows that look all ways, and air and sunshine galore. It was nursery first and then playroom and gymnasium, I should judge; for the windows are barred for little children, and there are rings and things in the walls.

The paint and paper look as if a boys' school had used it. It is stripped off — the paper — in great patches all around the head of my bed, about as far as I can reach, and in a great place on the other side of the room low down. I never saw a worse paper in my life.

One of those sprawling flamboyant patterns committing every artistic sin.

It is dull enough to confuse the eye in following, pronounced enough to constantly irritate and provoke study, and when you follow the lame uncertain curves for a little distance they suddenly commit suicide — plunge off at outrageous angles, destroy themselves in unheard of contradictions.

The color is repellant, almost revolting; a smouldering unclean yellow, strangely faded by the slow-turning sunlight.

It is a dull yet lurid orange in some places, a sickly sulphur tint in others.

No wonder the children hated it! I should hate it myself if I had to live in this room long.

There comes John, and I must put this away, — he hates to have me write a word.

★ ★ ★

We have been here two weeks, and I haven't felt like writing before, since that first day.

I am sitting by the window now, up in this atrocious nursery, and there is nothing to hinder my writing as much as I please, save lack of strength.

John is away all day, and even some nights when his cases are serious.

7

I am glad my case is not serious!

But these nervous troubles are dreadfully depressing.

John does not know how much I really suffer. He knows there is no *reason* to suffer, and that satisfies him.

Of course it is only nervousness. It does weigh on me so not to do my duty in any way!

I meant to be such a help to John, such a real rest and comfort, and here I am a comparative burden already!

Nobody would believe what an effort it is to do what little I am able, — to dress and entertain, and order things.

It is fortunate Mary is so good with the baby. Such a dear baby!

And yet I *cannot* be with him, it makes me so nervous.

I suppose John never was nervous in his life. He laughs at me so about this wall-paper!

At first he meant to repaper the room, but afterwards he said that I was letting it get the better of me, and that nothing was worse for a nervous patient than to give way to such fancies.

He said that after the wall-paper was changed it would be the heavy bedstead, and then the barred windows, and then that gate at the head of the stairs, and so on.

'You know the place is doing you good,' he

said, 'and really, dear, I don't care to renovate the house just for a three months' rental.'

'Then do let us go downstairs,' I said, 'there are such pretty rooms there.'

Then he took me in his arms and called me a blessed little goose, and said he would go down cellar, if I wished, and have it white-washed into the bargain.

But he is right enough about the beds and windows and things.

It is an airy and comfortable room as any one need wish, and, of course, I would not be so silly as to make him uncomfortable just for a whim.

I'm really getting quite fond of the big room, all but that horrid paper.

Out of one window I can see the garden, those mysterious deep-shaded arbors, the riotous old-fashioned flowers, and bushes and gnarly trees.

Out of another I get a lovely view of the bay and a little private wharf belonging to the estate. There is a beautiful shaded lane that runs down there from the house. I always fancy I see people walking in these numerous paths and arbors, but John has cautioned me not to give way to fancy in the least. He says that with my imaginative power and habit of story-making, a nervous weakness like mine is sure to lead to all manner of excited fancies, and that I ought to use my will and good sense to check the tendency. So I try.

I think sometimes that if I were only well enough to write a little it would relieve the press of ideas and rest me.

But I find I get pretty tired when I try.

It is so discouraging not to have any advice and companionship about my work. When I get really well, John says we will ask Cousin Henry and Julia down for a long visit; but he says he would as soon put fireworks in my pillow-case as to let me have those stimulating people about now.

I wish I could get well faster.

But I must not think about that. This paper looks to me as if it *knew* what a vicious influence it had!

There is a recurrent spot where the pattern lolls like a broken neck and two bulbous eyes stare at you upside down.

I get positively angry with the impertinence of it and the everlastingess. Up and down and sideways they crawl, and those absurd, unblinking eyes are everywhere. There is one place where two breadths didn't match, and the eyes go all up and down the line, one a little higher than the other.

I never saw so much expression in an inanimate thing before, and we all know how much expression they have! I used to lie awake as a child and get more entertainment and terror out of blank walls and plain furniture than most children could find in a toy-store.

I remember what a kindly wink the knobs of our big, old bureau used to have, and there was one chair that always seemed like a strong friend.

I used to feel that if any of the other things looked too fierce I could always hop into that chair and be safe.

The furniture in this room is no worse than inharmonious, however, for we had to bring it all from downstairs. I suppose when this was used as a playroom they had to take the nursery things out, and no wonder! I never saw such ravages as the children have made here.

The wall-paper, as I said before, is torn off in spots, and it sticketh closer than a brother — they must have had perseverance as well as hatred.

Then the floor is scratched and gouged and splintered, the plaster itself is dug out here and there, and this great heavy bed which is all we found in the room, looks as if it had been through the wars.

But I don't mind it a bit — only the paper.

There comes John's sister. Such a dear girl as she is, and so careful of me! I must not let her find me writing.

She is a perfect and enthusiastic house-keeper, and hopes for no better profession. I verily believe she thinks it is the writing which made me sick!

But I can write when she is out, and see her a long way off from these windows.

There is one that commands the road, a lovely shaded winding road, and one that just looks off over the country. A lovely country, too, full of great elms and velvet meadows.

This wall-paper has a kind of subpattern in a different shade, a particularly irritating one, for you can only see it in certain lights, and not clearly then.

But in the places where it isn't faded and where the sun is just so — I can see a strange, provoking, formless sort of figure, that seems to skulk about behind that silly and conspicuous front design.

There's sister on the stairs!

★   ★   ★

Well, the Fourth of July is over! The people are all gone and I am tired out. John thought it might do me good to see a little company, so we just had mother and Nellie and the children down for a week.

Of course I didn't do a thing. Jennie sees to everything now.

But it tired me all the same.

John says if I don't pick up faster he shall send me to Weir Mitchell in the fall.

But I don't want to go there at all. I had a friend who was in his hands once, and she says he is just like John and my brother, only more so!

Besides, it is such an undertaking to go so far.

I don't feel as if it was worth while to turn my hand over for anything, and I'm getting dreadfully fretful and querulous.

I cry at nothing, and cry most of the time.

Of course I don't when John is here, or anybody else, but when I am alone.

And I am alone a good deal just now. John is kept in town very often by serious cases, and Jennie is good and lets me alone when I want her to.

So I walk a little in the garden or down that lovely lane, sit on the porch under the roses, and lie down up here a good deal.

I'm getting really fond of the room in spite of the wall-paper. Perhaps *because* of the wall-paper.

It dwells in my mind so!

I lie here on this great immovable bed — it is nailed down, I believe — and follow that pattern about by the hour. It is as good as gymnastics, I assure you. I start, we'll say, at the bottom, down in the corner over there where it has not been touched, and I determine for the thousandth time that I *will* follow that pointless pattern to some sort of a conclusion.

I know a little of the principle of design, and I know this thing was not arranged on any laws of radiation, or alternation, or repetition, or symmetry, or anything else that I ever heard of.

It is repeated, of course, by the breadths, but not otherwise.

Looked at in one way each breadth stands alone, the bloated curves and flourishes — a kind of 'debased Romanesque' with *delirium tremens* — go waddling up and down in isolated columns of fatuity.

But, on the other hand, they connect diagonally, and the sprawling outlines run off in great slanting waves of optic horror, like a lot of wallowing seaweeds in full chase.

The whole thing goes horizontally, too, at least it seems so, and I exhaust myself in trying to distinguish the order of its going in that direction.

They have used a horizontal breadth for a frieze, and that adds wonderfully to the confusion.

There is one end of the room where it is almost intact, and there, when the crosslights fade and the low sun shines directly upon it, I can almost fancy radiation after all, — the interminable grotesque seem to form around a common centre and rush off in headlong plunges of equal distraction.

It makes me tired to follow it. I will take a nap I guess.

★   ★   ★

I don't know why I should write this.

I don't want to.

I don't feel able.

And I know John would think it absurd. But I *must* say what I feel and think in some way — it is such a relief!

But the effort is getting to be greater than the relief.

Half the time now I am awfully lazy, and lie down ever so much.

John says I mustn't lose my strength, and has me take cod liver oil and lots of tonics and things, to say nothing of ale and wine and rare meat.

Dear John! He loves me very dearly, and hates to have me sick. I tried to have a real earnest reasonable talk with him the other day, and tell him how I wish he would let me go and make a visit to Cousin Henry and Julia.

15

But he said I wasn't able to go, nor able to stand it after I got there; and I did not make out a very good case for myself, for I was crying before I had finished.

It is getting to be a great effort for me to think straight. Just this nervous weakness I suppose.

And dear John gathered me up in his arms, and just carried me upstairs and laid me on the bed, and sat by me and read to me till it tired my head.

He said I was his darling and his comfort and all he had, and that I must take care of myself for his sake, and keep well.

He says no one but myself can help me out of it, that I must use my will and self-control and not let any silly fancies run away with me.

There's one comfort: the baby is well and happy, and does not have to occupy this nursery with the horrid wall-paper.

If we had not used it, that blessed child would have! What a fortunate escape! Why, I wouldn't have a child of mine, an impressionable little thing, live in such a room for worlds.

I never thought of it before, but it is lucky that John kept me here after all, I can stand it so much easier than a baby, you see.

Of course I never mention it to them any more — I am too wise, — but I keep watch of it all the same.

16

There are things in that paper that nobody knows but me, or ever will.

Behind that outside pattern the dim shapes get clearer every day.

It is always the same shape, only very numerous.

And it is like a woman stooping down and creeping about behind that pattern. I don't like it a bit. I wonder — I begin to think — I wish John would take me away from here!

★   ★   ★

It is so hard to talk with John about my case because he is so wise, and because he loves me so.

But I tried it last night.

It was moonlight. The moon shines in all around just as the sun does.

I hate to see it sometimes, it creeps so slowly, and always comes in by one window or another.

John was asleep and I hated to waken him, so I kept still and watched the moonlight on that undulating wall-paper till I felt creepy.

The faint figure behind seemed to shake the pattern, just as if she wanted to get out.

I got up softly and went to feel and see if the paper *did* move, and when I came back John was awake.

'What is it, little girl?' he said. 'Don't go

17

walking about like that — you'll get cold.'

I thought it was a good time to talk, so I told him that I really was not gaining here, and that I wished he would take me away.

'Why, darling!' said he, 'our lease will be up in three weeks, and I can't see how to leave before.

'The repairs are not done at home, and I cannot possibly leave town just now. Of course if you were in any danger, I could and would, but you really are better, dear, whether you can see it or not. I am a doctor, dear, and I know. You are gaining flesh and color, your appetite is better, I feel really much easier about you.'

'I don't weigh a bit more,' said I, 'nor as much; and my appetite may be better in the evening when you are here, but it is worse in the morning when you are away!'

'Bless her little heart!' said he with a big hug, 'she shall be as sick as she pleases! But now let's improve the shining hours by going to sleep, and talk about it in the morning!'

'And you won't go away?' I asked gloomily.

'Why, how can I, dear? It is only three weeks more and then we will take a nice little trip of a few days while Jennie is getting the house ready. Really dear you are better!'

'Better in body perhaps — ' I began, and stopped short, for he sat up straight and looked at me with such a stern, reproachful look that I could not say another word.

'My darling,' said he, 'I beg of you, for my sake and for our child's sake, as well as for your own, that you will never for one instant let that idea enter your mind! There is nothing so dangerous, so fascinating, to a temperament like yours. It is a false and foolish fancy. Can you not trust me as a physician when I tell you so?'

So of course I said no more on that score, and we went to sleep before long. He thought I was asleep first, but I wasn't, and lay there for hours trying to decide whether that front pattern and the back pattern really did move together or separately.

★ ★ ★

On a pattern like this, by daylight, there is a lack of sequence, a defiance of law, that is a constant irritant to a normal mind.

The color is hideous enough, and unreliable enough, and infuriating enough, but the pattern is torturing.

You think you have mastered it, but just as you get well underway in following, it turns a back-somersault and there you are. It slaps you in the face, knocks you down, and tramples upon you. It is like a bad dream.

19

The outside pattern is a florid arabesque, reminding one of a fungus. If you can imagine a toadstool in joints, an interminable string of toadstools, budding and sprouting in endless convolutions — why, that is something like it.

That is, sometimes!

There is one marked peculiarity about this paper, a thing nobody seems to notice but myself, and that is that it changes as the light changes.

When the sun shoots in through the east window — I always watch for that first long, straight ray — it changes so quickly that I never can quite believe it.

That is why I watch it always.

By moonlight — the moon shines in all night when there is a moon — I wouldn't know it was the same paper.

At night in any kind of light, in twilight, candlelight, lamplight, and worst of all by moonlight, it becomes bars! The outside pattern I mean, and the woman behind it is as plain as can be.

I didn't realize for a long time what the thing was that showed behind, that dim sub-pattern, but now I am quite sure it is a woman.

By daylight she is subdued, quiet. I fancy it is the pattern that keeps her so still. It is so puzzling. It keeps me quiet by the hour.

I lie down ever so much now. John says it is good for me, and to sleep all I can.

Indeed he started the habit by making me lie down for an hour after each meal.

It is a very bad habit I am convinced, for you see I don't sleep.

And that cultivates deceit, for I don't tell them I'm awake — O no!

The fact is I am getting a little afraid of John.

He seems very queer sometimes, and even Jennie has an inexplicable look.

It strikes me occasionally, just as a scientific hypothesis, — that perhaps it is the paper!

I have watched John when he did not know I was looking, and come into the room suddenly on the most innocent excuses, and I've caught him several times *looking at the paper!* And Jennie too. I caught Jennie with her hand on it once.

She didn't know I was in the room, and when I asked her in a quiet, a very quiet voice, with the most restrained manner possible, what she was doing with the paper — she turned around as if she had been caught stealing, and looked quite angry — asked me why I should frighten her so!

Then she said that the paper stained everything it touched, that she had found yellow smooches on all my clothes and John's, and she wished we would be more careful!

Did not that sound innocent? But I know she was studying that pattern, and I am determined that nobody shall find it out but myself!

* ★ ★

Life is very much more exciting now than it used to be. You see I have something more to expect, to look forward to, to watch. I really do eat better, and am more quiet than I was.

John is so pleased to see me improve! He laughed a little the other day, and said I seemed to be flourishing in spite of my wall-paper.

I turned it off with a laugh. I had no intention of telling him it was *because* of the wall-paper — he would make fun of me. He might even want to take me away.

I don't want to leave now until I have found it out. There is a week more, and I think that will be enough.

* ★ ★

I'm feeling ever so much better! I don't sleep much at night, for it is so interesting to watch developments; but I sleep a good deal in the daytime.

In the daytime it is tiresome and perplexing.

There are always new shoots on the fungus, and new shades of yellow all over it. I cannot keep count of them, though I have tried conscientiously.

It is the strangest yellow, that wall-paper! It makes me think of all the yellow things I ever saw — not beautiful ones like buttercups, but old foul, bad yellow things.

But there is something else about that paper — the smell! I noticed it the moment we came into the room, but with so much air and sun it was not bad. Now we have had a week of fog and rain, and whether the windows are open or not, the smell is here.

It creeps all over the house.

I find it hovering in the dining-room, skulking in the parlor, hiding in the hall, lying in wait for me on the stairs.

It gets into my hair.

Even when I go to ride, if I turn my head suddenly and surprise it — there is that smell!

Such a peculiar odor, too! I have spent hours in trying to analyze it, to find what it smelled like.

It is not bad — at first, and very gentle, but quite the subtlest, most enduring odor I ever met.

In this damp weather it is awful, I wake up in the night and find it hanging over me.

It used to disturb me at first. I thought seriously of burning the house — to reach the smell.

But now I am used to it. The only thing I can think of that it is like is the *color* of the paper! A yellow smell.

There is a very funny mark on this wall, low down, near the mopboard. A streak that runs round the room. It goes behind every piece of furniture, except the bed, a long, straight, even *smooch*, as if it had been rubbed over and over.

I wonder how it was done and who did it, and what they did it for. Round and round and round — round and round and round — it makes me dizzy!

★ ★ ★

I really have discovered something at last.

Through watching so much at night, when it changes so, I have finally found out.

The front pattern *does* move — and no wonder! The woman behind shakes it!

Sometimes I think there are a great many women behind, and sometimes only one, and she crawls around fast, and her crawling shakes it all over.

Then in the very bright spots she keeps still, and in the very shady spots she just takes

24

hold of the bars and shakes them hard.

And she is all the time trying to climb through. But nobody could climb through that pattern — it strangles so; I think that is why it has so many heads.

They get through, and then the pattern strangles them off and turns them upside down, and makes their eyes white!

If those heads were covered or taken off it would not be half so bad.

★ ★ ★

I think that woman gets out in the daytime!

And I'll tell you why — privately — I've seen her!

I can see her out of every one of my windows!

It is the same woman, I know, for she is always creeping, and most women do not creep by daylight.

I see her in that long shaded lane, creeping up and down. I see her in those dark grape arbors, creeping all around the garden.

I see her on that long road under the trees, creeping along, and when a carriage comes she hides under the blackberry vines.

I don't blame her a bit. It must be very humiliating to be caught creeping by daylight!

I always lock the door when I creep by

daylight. I can't do it at night, for I know John would suspect something at once.

And John is so queer now, that I don't want to irritate him. I wish he would take another room! Besides, I don't want anybody to get that woman out at night but myself.

I often wonder if I could see her out of all the windows at once.

But, turn as fast as I can, I can only see out of one at one time.

And though I always see her, she *may* be able to creep faster than I can turn!

I have watched her sometimes away off in the open country, creeping as fast as a cloud shadow in a high wind.

★   ★   ★

If only that top pattern could be gotten off from the under one! I mean to try it, little by little.

I have found out another funny thing, but I shan't tell it this time! It does not do to trust people too much.

There are only two more days to get this paper off, and I believe John is beginning to notice. I don't like the look in his eyes.

And I heard him ask Jennie a lot of professional questions about me. She had a very good report to give.

26

She said I slept a good deal in the daytime.

John knows I don't sleep very well at night, for all I'm so quiet!

He asked me all sorts of questions, too, and pretended to be very loving and kind.

As if I couldn't see through him!

Still, I don't wonder he acts so, sleeping under this paper for three months.

It only interests me, but I feel sure John and Jennie are secretly affected by it.

★ ★ ★

Hurrah! This is the last day, but it is enough. John to stay in town over night, and won't be out until this evening.

Jennie wanted to sleep with me — the sly thing! but I told her I should undoubtedly rest better for a night all alone.

That was clever, for really I wasn't alone a bit! As soon as it was moonlight and that poor thing began to crawl and shake the pattern, I got up and ran to help her.

I pulled and she shook, I shook and she pulled, and before morning we had peeled off yards of that paper.

A strip about as high as my head and half around the room.

And then when the sun came and that awful pattern began to laugh at me, I declared I would finish it to-day!

We go away to-morrow, and they are moving all my furniture down again to leave things as they were before.

Jennie looked at the wall in amazement, but I told her merrily that I did it out of pure spite at the vicious thing.

She laughed and said she wouldn't mind doing it herself, but I must not get tired.

How she betrayed herself that time!

But I am here, and no person touches this paper but me, — not *alive!*

She tried to get me out of the room — it was too patent! But I said it was so quiet and empty and clean now that I believed I would lie down again and sleep all I could; and not to wake me even for dinner — I would call when I woke.

So now she is gone, and the servants are gone, and the things are gone, and there is nothing left but that great bedstead nailed down, with the canvas mattress we found on it.

We shall sleep downstairs to-night, and take the boat home to-morrow.

I quite enjoy the room, now it is bare again.

How those children did tear about here!

This bedstead is fairly gnawed!

But I must get to work.

I have locked the door and thrown the key

down into the front path.

I don't want to go out, and I don't want to have anybody come in, till John comes.

I want to astonish him.

I've got a rope up here that even Jennie did not find. If that woman does get out, and tries to get away, I can tie her!

But I forgot I could not reach far without anything to stand on!

This bed will *not* move!

I tried to lift and push it until I was lame, and then I got so angry I bit off a little piece at one corner — but it hurt my teeth.

Then I peeled off all the paper I could reach standing on the floor. It sticks horribly and the pattern just enjoys it! All those strangled heads and bulbous eyes and waddling fungus growths just shriek with derision!

I am getting angry enough to do something desperate. To jump out of the window would be admirable exercise, but the bars are too strong even to try.

Besides I wouldn't do it. Of course not. I know well enough that a step like that is improper and might be misconstrued.

I don't like to *look* out of the windows even — there are so many of those creeping women, and they creep so fast.

I wonder if they all come out of that

wall-paper as I did?

But I am securely fastened now by my well-hidden rope — you don't get *me* out in the road there!

I suppose I shall have to get back behind the pattern when it comes night, and that is hard!

It is so pleasant to be out in this great room and creep around as I please!

I don't want to go outside. I won't, even if Jennie asks me to.

For outside you have to creep on the ground, and everything is green instead of yellow.

But here I can creep smoothly on the floor, and my shoulder just fits in that long smooch around the wall, so I cannot lose my way.

Why there's John at the door!

It is no use, young man, you can't open it!

How he does call and pound!

Now he's crying for an axe.

It would be a shame to break down that beautiful door!

'John dear!' said I in the gentlest voice, 'the key is down by the front steps, under a plantain leaf!'

That silenced him for a few moments.

Then he said — very quietly indeed, 'Open the door, my darling!'

'I can't,' said I. 'The key is down by the

front door under a plantain leaf!'

And then I said it again, several times, very gently and slowly, and said it so often that he had to go and see, and he got it of course, and came in. He stopped short by the door.

'What is the matter?' he cried. 'For God's sake, what are you doing!'

I kept on creeping just the same, but I looked at him over my shoulder.

'I've got out at last,' said I, 'in spite of you and Jennie! And I've pulled off most of the paper, so you can't put me back!'

Now why should that man have fainted? But he did, and right across my path by the wall, so that I had to creep over him every time!

According to Solomon

''He that rebuketh a man afterwards shall find more favor than he that flattereth with his tongue,'' said Mr Solomon Bankside to his wife Mary.

'It's the other way with a woman, I think;' she answered him, 'you might put that in.'

'Tut, tut, Molly,' said he; ''Add not unto his words,' — do not speak lightly of the wisdom of the great king.'

'I don't mean to, dear, but — when you hear it all the time — '

''He that turneth away his ear from the law, even his prayer shall be an abomination,'' answered Mr Bankside.

'I believe you know every one of those old Proverbs by heart,' said his wife with some heat. 'Now that's *not* disrespectful! — they *are* old! — and I do wish you'd forget some of them!'

He smiled at her quizzically, tossing back his heavy silver-gray hair with the gesture she had always loved. His eyes were deep blue and bright under their bushy brows; and the mouth was kind — in its iron way. 'I can think of at least three to squelch you with,

Molly,' said he, 'but I won't.'

'O I know the one you want! 'A continual dropping in a very rainy day and a contentious woman are alike!' I'm *not* contentious, Solomon!'

'No, you are not,' he frankly admitted. 'What I really had in mind was this — 'A prudent wife is from the Lord,' and 'He that findeth a wife findeth a good thing; and obtaineth favor of the Lord.''

She ran around the table in the impulsive way years did not alter, and kissed him warmly.

'I'm not scolding you, my dear,' he continued; 'but if you had all the money you'd like to give away — there wouldn't be much left!'

'But look at what you spend on me!' she urged.

'That's a wise investment — as well as a deserved reward,' her husband answered calmly. ''There is that scattereth and yet increaseth,' you know, my dear; 'And there is that withholdeth more than is meet — and it tendeth to poverty!' Take all you get my dear — it's none too good for you.'

He gave her his goodbye kiss with special fondness, put on his heavy satin-lined overcoat and went to the office.

Mr Solomon Bankside was not a Jew; though his last name suggested and his first seemed to prove it; also his proficiency in the Old Testament gave color to the idea. No; he came from Vermont; of generations of unbroken New England and old English Puritan ancestry, where the Solomons and Isaacs and Zedekiahs were only mitigated by the Standfasts and Praise-the-Lords. Pious, persistent pig-headed folk were they, down all the line.

His wife had no such simple pedigree. A streak of Huguenot blood she had (some of the best in France, though neither of them knew that), a grandmother from Albany with a Van to her name; a great grandmother with a Mac; and another with an O'; even a German cross came in somewhere. Mr Bankside was devoted to genealogy, and had been at some pains to dig up these facts — the more he found the worse he felt, and the lower ran his opinion of Mrs Bankside's ancestry.

She had been a fascinating girl; pretty, with the dash and piquancy of an oriole in a May apple-tree; clever and efficient in everything her swift hands touched; quite a spectacular housekeeper; and the sober, long-faced young downeasterner had married her with a sudden decision that he often wondered about in later years. So did she.

What he had not sufficiently weighed at the

time, was her spirit of incorrigible independence, and a light-mindedness which, on
maturer judgment, he could almost term
irreligious. His conduct was based on principle, all of it; built firmly into habit and
buttressed by scriptural quotations. Hers
seemed to him as inconsequent as the flight
of a moth. Studying it, in his solemn
conscientious way, in the light of his
genealogical researches, he felt that all her
uncertainties were accounted for, and that the
error was his — in having married too many
kinds of people at once.

They had been, and were, very happy
together none the less: though sometimes
their happiness was a little tottery. This was
one of the times. It was the day after
Christmas, and Mrs Bankside entered the big
drawing room, redolent of popcorn and
evergreen, and walked slowly to the corner
where the fruits of yesterday were lovingly
arranged; so few that she had been able to
give — so many that she had received.

There were the numerous pretty inter-
changeable things given her by her many
friends; 'presents,' suitable to any lady. There
were the few perfectly selected ones given by
the few who knew her best. There was the
rather perplexing gift of Mrs MacAvelly.
There was her brother's stiff white envelope

enclosing a check. There were the loving gifts of children and grandchildren.

Finally there was Solomon's.

It was his custom to bestow upon her one solemn and expensive object, a boon as it were, carefully selected, after much thought and balancing of merits; but the consideration was spent on the nature of the gift — not on the desires of the recipient. There was the piano she could not play, the statue she did not admire, the set of Dante she never read, the heavy gold bracelet, the stiff diamond brooch — and all the others. This time it was a set of sables, costing even more than she imagined.

Christmas after Christmas had these things come to her; and she stood there now, thinking of that procession of unvalued valuables, with an expression so mixed and changeful it resembled a kaleidoscope. Love for Solomon, pride in Solomon, respect for Solomon's judgment and power to pay, gratitude for his unfailing kindness and generosity, impatience with his always giving her this one big valuable permanent thing, when he knew so well that she much preferred small renewable cheap ones; her personal dislike of furs, the painful conviction that brown was not becoming to her — all these and more filled the little woman with what used to be called 'conflicting emotions.'

She smoothed out her brother's check, wishing as she always did that it had come before Christmas, so that she might buy more presents for her beloved people. Solomon liked to spend money on her — in his own way; but he did not like to have her spend money on him — or on anyone for that matter. She had asked her brother once, if he would mind sending her his Christmas present beforehand.

'Not on your life, Polly!' he said. 'You'd never see a cent of it! You can't buy 'em many things right on top of Christmas, and it'll be gone long before the next one.'

She put the check away and turned to examine her queerest gift. Upon which scrutiny presently entered the donor.

'I'm ever so much obliged, Benigna,' said Mrs Bankside. 'You know how I love to do things. It's a loom, isn't it? Can you show me how it works?'

'Of course I can, my dear; that's just what I ran in for — I was afraid you wouldn't know. But you are so clever with your hands that I'm sure you'll enjoy it. I do.'

Whereat Mrs MacAvelly taught Mrs Bankside the time-honored art of weaving. And Mrs Bankside enjoyed it more than any previous handicraft she had essayed.

She did it well, beginning with rather coarse and simple weaves; and gradually learning the finer grades of work. Despising as she did the more modern woolens, she bought real wool yarn of a lovely red — and made some light warm flannelly stuff in which she proceeded to rapturously enclose her little grandchildren.

Mr Bankside warmly approved, murmuring affectionately, ''She seeketh wool and flax — she worketh willingly with her hands.''

He watched little Bob and Polly strenuously 'helping' the furnace man to clear the sidewalk, hopping about like red-birds in their new caps and coats; and his face beamed with the appositeness of his quotation, as he remarked, ''She is not afraid of the snow for her household, for all her household are clothed with scarlet!'' and he proffered an extra, wholly spontaneous kiss, which pleased her mightily.

'You dear man!' she said with a hug; 'I believe you'd rather find a proverb to fit than a gold mine!'

To which he triumphantly responded: ''Wisdom is better than rubies; and all the things that may be desired are not to be compared to it.''

She laughed sweetly at him. 'And do you think wisdom stopped with that string of proverbs?'

'You can't get much beyond it,' he

answered calmly. 'If we lived up to all there is in that list we shouldn't be far out, my dear!'

Whereat she laughed again, smoothed his gray mane, and kissed him in the back of his neck. 'You *dear* thing!' said Mrs Bankside.

She kept herself busy with the new plaything as he called it. Hands that had been rather empty were now smoothly full. Her health was better, and any hint of occasional querulousness disappeared entirely; so that her husband was moved to fresh admiration of her sunny temper, and quoted for the hundredth time, ''She openeth her mouth with wisdom, and in her tongue is the law of kindness.''

Mrs MacAvelly taught her to make towels. But Mrs Bankside's skill outstripped hers; she showed inventive genius and designed patterns of her own. The fineness and quality of the work increased; and she joyfully replenished her linen chest with her own handiwork.

'I tell you, my dear,' said Mrs MacAvelly, 'if you'd be willing to sell them you could get almost *any* price for those towels. With the initials woven in. I know I could get you orders — through the Woman's Exchange, you know!'

Mrs Bankside was delighted. 'What fun!' she said. 'And I needn't appear at all?'

'No, you needn't appear at all — do let me try.'

So Mrs Bankside made towels of price, soft, fine, and splendid, till she was weary of them; and in the opulence of constructive genius fell to devising woven belts of elaborate design.

These were admired excessively. All her women friends wanted one, or more; the Exchange got hold of it, there was a distinct demand; and finally Mrs MacAvelly came in one day with a very important air and a special order.

'I don't know what you'll think, my dear,' she said, 'but I happen to know the Percys very well — the big store people, you know; and Mr Percy was talking about those belts of yours to me; — of course he didn't know they are yours; but he said (the Exchange people told him I knew, you see), 'If you can place an order with that woman, I can take all she'll make and pay her full price for them. Is she poor?' he asked. 'Is she dependent on her work?' And I told him, 'Not altogether.' And I think he thinks it an interesting case! Anyhow, there's the order. Will you do it?'

Mrs Bankside was much excited. She wanted to very much, but dreaded offending her husband. So far she had not told him of her quiet trade in towels; but hid and saved this precious money — the first she had ever earned.

The two friends discussed the pros and cons at considerable length; and finally with some perturbation, she decided to accept the order.

'You'll never tell, Benigna!' she urged. 'Solomon would never forgive me, I'm afraid.'

'Why of course I won't — you needn't have a moment's fear of it. You give them to me — I'll stop with the carriage you see; and I take them to the Exchange — and he gets them from there.'

'It seems like smuggling!' said Mrs Bankside delightedly. 'I always did love to smuggle!'

'They say women have no conscience about laws, don't they?' Mrs MacAvelly suggested.

'Why should we?' answered her friend. 'We don't make 'em — nor God — nor nature. Why on earth should we respect a set of silly rules made by some men one day and changed by some more the next?'

'Bless us, Polly! Do you talk to Mr Bankside like that?'

'Indeed I don't!' answered her hostess, holding out a particularly beautiful star-patterned belt to show to advantage. 'There are lots of things I don't say to Mr Bankside — 'A man of understanding holdeth his peace' you know — or a woman.'

She was a pretty creature, her hair like that of a powdered marchioness, her rosy cheeks and firm slight figure suggesting a charmer in Dresden china.

Mrs MacAvelly regarded her admiringly. ''Where there is no wood the fire goeth out; so where there is no tale bearer the strife ceaseth,'' she proudly offered, 'I can quote that much myself.'

But Mrs Bankside had many misgivings as she pursued her audacious way; the busy hours flying away from her, and the always astonishing checks flying toward her in gratifying accumulation. She came down to her well-planned dinners gracious and sweet; always effectively dressed; spent the cosy quiet evenings with her husband, or went out with him, with a manner of such increased tenderness and charm that his heart warmed anew to the wife of his youth; and he even relented a little toward her miscellaneous ancestors.

As the days shortened and darkened she sparkled more and more; with little snatches of song now and then; gay ineffectual strumming on the big piano; sudden affectionate darts at him, with quaintly distributed caresses.

'Molly!' said he, 'I don't believe you're a

day over twenty! What makes you act so?'

'Don't you like it, So?' she asked him. That was the nearest she ever would approximate to his name.

He did like it, naturally, and even gave her an extra ten dollars to buy Christmas presents with; while he meditated giving her an electric runabout; — to her! — who was afraid of a wheelbarrow!

When the day arrived and the family were gathered together, Mrs Bankside, wearing the diamond brooch, the gold bracelet, the point lace handkerchief — everything she could carry of his accumulated generosity — and such an air of triumphant mystery that the tree itself was dim beside her; handed out to her astonished relatives such an assortment of desirable articles that they found no words to express their gratitude.

'Why, *Mother!*' said Jessie, whose husband was a minister and salaried as such, 'Why, *Mother* — how did you know we wanted just that kind of a rug! — and a sewing-machine *too!* And this lovely suit — and — and — why *Mother!*'

But her son-in-law took her aside and kissed her solemnly. He had wanted that particular set of sociological books for years — and never hoped to get them; or that bunch of magazines either.

46

Nellie had 'married rich;' she was less ostentatiously favored; but she had shown her thankfulness a week ago — when her mother had handed her a check.

'Sh, sh! my dear!' her mother had said, 'Not one word. I know! What pleasant weather we're having.'

This son-in-law was agreeably surprised, too; and the other relatives, married and single; while the children rioted among their tools and toys, taking this Christmas like any other, as a season of unmitigated joy.

Mr Solomon Bankside looked on with growing amazement, making computations in his practiced mind; saying nothing whatever. Should he criticize his wife before others?

But when his turn came — when gifts upon gifts were offered to him — sets of silken handkerchiefs (he couldn't bear the touch of a silk handkerchief!), a cabinet of cards and chips and counters of all sorts (he never played cards), an inlaid chess-table and ivory men (the game was unknown to him), a gorgeous scarf-pin (he abominated jewelery), a five pound box of candy (he never ate it), his feelings so mounted within him, that since he would not express and could not repress them, he summarily went up stairs to his room.

She found him there later, coming in blushing, smiling, crying a little too — like a naughty but charming child.

He swallowed hard as he looked at her; and his voice was a little strained.

'I can take a joke as well as any man, Molly. I guess we're square on that. But — my dear! — where did you get it?'

'Earned it,' said she, looking down, and fingering her lace handkerchief.

'Earned it! My wife, earning money! How — if I may ask?'

'By my weaving, dear — the towels and the belts — I sold 'em. Don't be angry — nobody knows — my name didn't appear at all! Please don't be angry! — It isn't wicked, and it was such fun!'

'No — it's not wicked, I suppose,' said he rather grimly. 'But it is certainly a most mortifying and painful thing to me — most unprecedented.'

'Not so unprecedented, dear,' she urged, 'Even the woman you think most of did it! Don't you remember 'She maketh fine linen and selleth it — and delivereth girdles unto the merchants!''

Mr Bankside came down handsomely.

He got used to it after a while, and then he became proud of it. If a friend ventured to suggest a criticism, or to sympathize, he would calmly respond, ''The heart of her husband doth safely trust in her, so that he shall have no need of spoil. Give her of the fruit of her hands, and let her own works praise her in the gates.''

Circumstances Alter Cases

I

'Are you going to let a wretched prejudice like this stand against my love?' he asked; 'an empty impersonal sex-prejudice against a man's lifelong devotion? You say you love me, and yet you won't marry me because I don't agree with you in all your ideas! A pretty kind of love!'

'I am not defending my special variety of love,' she answered, slowly. 'I never pretended it was all absorbing, or everlasting, or in any way equal to a man's lifelong devotion. I am, unfortunately, one of those much-berated New England women who have learned to think as well as feel; and to me, at least, marriage means more than a union of hearts and bodies — it must mean minds, too. It would be a never-ending grief to me, starvation and bitter pain, to have you indifferent or contemptuous to my most earnest thoughts and beliefs. You see, I should love you enough to care.'

'Yes, I see! I see a great deal!' he replied, walking over to the hearth and leaning his arm against the mantel. He seemed to borrow fire from the glowing coals, for he came back and began again with restrained intensity:

'It is another instance of this cursed modern education! The women of to-day develop their minds until they are stronger than heart and body together — too strong to yield to a healthy love. And so they live, and so they die, and who is the better for it!'

'My dear George, you feel so keenly that it makes you unjust. You are not fair to women. It is that, more than anything else, which stands between us. If you are not fair now, to your heart's idol, your queen and all that, what *would* you be to your wife?'

She leaned back against the dull bronze green of the great chair, a lovely picture in the soft firelight, and looked at him steadily. Youth; health and beauty were in the up-turned face, and the free fine curves of body and limb showed that modern education had trained something besides intellect.

He turned over several things in his mind before replying. It was really difficult. Masculine habits of thought, dominant for centuries, were strong within him. He was a just man in most things, and he knew it. But his sense of chivalry and love for her moved him to soften what was most natural to say; and, under all, the individual soul could but admit some truth in her accusation.

'I can't talk any more on this theme to-night,' he said at last. 'But once convict me of an instance of clear injustice to your sex, and I will own you are right — and that it is wiser for us to live apart. Come, won't you sing to me a little before I go?'

'With all my heart,' said she. 'You see it is with all my heart, not my head, so we don't quarrel over music!'

He suppressed an impatient rejoinder, and they went to the piano.

II

George Saunders and his friend Howard Clarke — schoolmates, college chums, and partners at law — were strolling the beach next day below the high bluff where stood the imposing 'cottage' of Hilda Warde.

She was, as she had said, one of those New England women who are so disproportionately numerous that they cannot marry at home, while to take them away would go far toward depopulating the country.

They are a singular race. Violating every law of woman's existence according to the canons, they still live, and often present a favorable contrast to their married sisters in both health and happiness. As to usefulness, of course, they have none. No trifles in the way of personal achievement can counterbalance the delinquency of unmarried women. They live, and Hilda bade fair to finally join their ranks, for she was twenty-seven, travelled, cultured, experienced, and 'peculiar.'

Clarke had loved her, vainly, and gotten safely over it, much to his astonishment. Saunders had loved her at the same time, and did still — not wholly in vain, for she at least professed to love him; but still she would not marry.

'Howard,' he said, after they had strolled a gloomy mile, comforted only by their cigars, 'do you think she cares for me or not?'

'Doesn't she say so?' inquired Howard.

'Yes, she says so, but she doesn't act so. If a woman really loves, she doesn't hesitate over a matter of opinion. There isn't one woman in a hundred to-day, here at least, with a heart as big as a button! I am glad I am going abroad.'

'Have you made up your mind when to start?'

'I shall start to-night if I can't get anything more definite from Hilda. I'll take the early boat to Boston, and leave by the Wednesday steamer — the *Ithuriel*. I had a berth engaged with the privilege of countermanding, and only came down here in hopes — ' He broke off, and looked wearily out to sea.

'It's too bad, George!' cried Howard. 'There isn't a woman in christendom that's worth the sacrifice you are making! You would have been one of the first lawyers in the country before this, and nobody knows what politically, if you hadn't wasted these years on that heartless jilt! Look at that Ashford case you lost. I know why you lost it. Nothing on earth but sleeplessness and misery. It's as bad as murder! Talk about justice! If women got the justice they are so anxious for, there wouldn't be many of them left.'

'Stop!' said Saunders. 'She is a woman, and I love her. For my sake, be still.' And they were still for another gloomy mile, till they caught sight of Hilda herself, on the edge of the cliff above them, walking with a swift, free grace, her figure outlined clearly against the sky. She saw them presently, and began to descend a steep little path, motioning back their start to help her.

'I was coming down anyway,' she said, 'and, besides, it is easier for one to come down than for two to come up. But I want to rest a moment, for I've been to Shark Rock, and then a story to tell and an opinion to ask.'

They ensconced themselves in a shaded and windless corner, and Miss Warde was about to begin, when she espied a new-made friend of theirs, somewhat a lion in the little place, standing uncertainly a short way off, his hat in his hand.

He was a young Russian, wealthy, noble, and famous in his own country, but now a lifelong exile, making a tool of what had been a weapon before — his pen.

'Won't you join us, Count Stefan?' asked Hilda. 'I want an audience to-day.'

So the three gentlemen, after a moment's talk, settled themselves at her feet and she began her story.

'It is only a little one,' she said, 'but a true story; and I want your honest opinions on the merits of the case. *Honest* — mind you!

'There was a young man, good and clever and all that, but a little queer and opinionated. He had great notions of the work he was going to do, and really showed some promise, though nobody believed in his reformatory ideas or his ability either — he was so indefinite. Well, he met a young woman.'

'Of course,' remarked Saunders.

'Fate!' said Clarke.

'He was fortunate,' murmured the Count.

'Now, you must not interrupt,' frowned Hilda. 'This is a test case, and I want your calmest judgment. This young woman fell in love with him, and — I won't say made up her mind, for that was not her method — but she wanted to marry him. She was a fine girl, handsome and clever, a genius in her line. She was musical, and they might have been great friends but for that. But he was a rabid reformer, and she cared for nothing but love and music; so he didn't want to marry her, though he could not but love her in a way, she was so good and beautiful and — well, a strongly feminine nature.

'They were intimate friends and talked with all the freedom of the philosopher on one side and the artist on the other. He found out how things were going, and told her freely his plans and hopes; how he was resolved never to marry, that she was to him but a dear friend — everything as clear as daylight.

'But our young woman had her own plans and hopes. To do her justice, she didn't believe in his projects at all, and felt sure she could make him both powerful and happy by marrying him; so she went to work. Her methods were simple. She just took advantage of the freedom of their friendship to play upon his masculine nature. She had no scruples of any kind in such a case. She loved him, and him alone, and meant to marry him — that was all.

'Of course, it was only a matter of time. He struggled manfully, made engagements and broke them, left her and returned again; she always managed, by appealing to sympathy or friendship, or by a blank, reproachful silence, to get him to come and see her once more. After a while he felt his honor was engaged, and then he stuck to it, and married her. He loved her somewhat, you understand, through it all; only he knew — '

'Knew what?' from the Count, whose quiet eyes never left her face.

'Knew how it would end.'

'How did it end?' asked Saunders, rather bitterly.

'Just as he feared. It upset his work and health and everything. He wasn't earning much anyway, and that bothered him, as it always does. There was a child, of course; and between the extra care and unusual demands, and the miserable state of mind he was in, it quite ruined him. He just went insane and killed himself — one of those excitable, nervous temperaments, you know.

'That's all the story. What I want of you gentlemen is an opinion on the relative guilt of the two parties.'

'Guilt of the one party, you mean,' said Saunders, harshly. 'He was weak, no doubt — most men are in a similar case — but she was the one to blame!'

'She didn't force him to marry her,' objected Hilda, mildly. 'He might have escaped or refused.'

'And where could he have gone, pray, to escape a hunter like that — even if he had the means, which I understand he hadn't? And as to refusing — she led him on till he *couldn't* refuse — in honor! No, indeed. Get a man into the hands of a woman like that, and he can neither escape nor refuse.'

'I agree with George,' said Howard Clarke. 'The girl was altogether to blame.'

'Do I understand,' inquired the Count, with his perfect accent, 'that she made the proposal of marriage?'

'She did,' said Hilda.

'And that he explained to her that he did not love her in that way, and that he was unfit and unwilling to marry?'

'Clearly and repeatedly,' said Hilda.

'And that, after being led into one engagement, he broke it and left her, only to be pulled back again?'

'He did.'

'I am forced to agree with these gentlemen against the lady. She was most cruelly to blame.'

Hilda's eyes dwelt on him a moment admiringly, as he uttered the quiet but impressive syllables. Then she studied the other speakers.

'It makes no difference in a case like that,' Saunders broke out, 'whether it's a man or a woman. To play on a person like that and win him against his will through his worst and weakest nature! She was a criminal!'

'But she loved him,' said Hilda.

'Love! Do you call *that* love? To ruin a man's life!' Mr Saunders's horror overcame him and he became speechless.

Hilda Warde sat quiet for a few minutes. 'And you, Mr Clarke?'

'Of course I say the same. Sorry, to a woman, but she was a selfish wretch!'

Hilda heaved a long sigh.

'Well, my friends,' she said at length, 'I hope you are honest. I have made one error in my story — just a trifle. The facts are all the same, but the sexes are reversed. It is the story of my friend May Henderson and her husband.'

The Count looked mildly surprised, and seemed trying to rebuild the tale on the new basis in his mind.

But Saunders spoke out vehemently.

'Why, Hilda, it's not the same case at all. John Henderson's a capital fellow — a real genius. And his wife was a nervous hypochondriac. It was the kindest thing she ever did — her departure.'

Hilda regarded him softly with her great brown eyes.

'But she used to be a paragon of health, and of most brilliant promise. And she told him she did not wish to marry — was not able or willing.'

Saunders laughed scornfully.

'Plenty of girls would say that,' he answered. 'She was a beautiful creature, and he had a perfect right to marry her if he could. She need not let him if she really did not want to — it's a free country!'

'I am so glad it is a free country,' said Hilda, rising. 'I am quite satisfied with your answer, George. Don't you think it will do for that single instance you mentioned last night?'

'I see,' he replied, in a restrained voice. 'A very pretty little trap!'

'It's a wholly different matter when you change the sex,' cried Mr Clarke, vehemently. 'It alters — er — everything!'

'So I see,' said Hilda.

'But, madame,' the Count quietly interposed, 'you say the tale remains the same — identical?'

'Exactly the same, Count Stefan.'

'Then surely the judgment is the same — the man was so the criminal!'

'Excuse me — I must bid you good-bye,' here broke in Mr Saunders. 'I am going to Boston to-night, and sail Wednesday, as I told you. Howard is going to walk down with me.'

The farewells were soon said, and somewhat coldly.

'Shall we not go back together?' asked Mr Clarke, seeing her also preparing to start.

'Thank you, no,' said she, 'I am going by the upper path.'

'May I accompany you?' asked the Count.

'If you care for climbing — and a high wind,' she answered.

And they went together.

The Giant Wistaria

'Meddle not with my new vine, child! See! Thou hast already broken the tender shoot! Never needle or distaff for thee, and yet thou wilt not be quiet!'

The nervous fingers wavered, clutched at a small carnelian cross that hung from her neck, then fell despairingly.

'Give me my child, mother, and then I will be quiet!'

'Hush! hush! thou fool — some one might be near! See — there is thy father coming, even now! Get in quickly!'

She raised her eyes to her mother's face, weary eyes that yet had a flickering, uncertain blaze in their shaded depths.

'Art thou a mother and hast no pity on me, a mother? Give me my child!'

Her voice rose in a strange, low cry, broken by her father's hand upon her mouth.

'Shameless!' said he, with set teeth. 'Get to thy chamber, and be not seen again to-night, or I will have thee bound!'

She went at that, and a hard-faced serving woman followed, and presently returned, bringing a key to her mistress.

'Is all well with her, — and the child also?'

'She is quiet, Mistress Dwining, well for the night, be sure. The child fretteth endlessly, but save for that it thriveth with me.'

The parents were left alone together on the high square porch with its great pillars, and the rising moon began to make faint shadows of the young vine leaves that shot up luxuriantly around them; moving shadows, like little stretching fingers, on the broad and heavy planks of the oaken floor.

'It groweth well, this vine thou broughtest me in the ship, my husband.'

'Aye,' he broke in bitterly, 'and so doth the shame I brought thee! Had I known of it I would sooner have had the ship founder beneath us, and have seen our child cleanly drowned, than live to this end!'

'Thou art very hard, Samuel, art thou not afeard for her life? She grieveth sore for the child, aye, and for the green fields to walk in!'

'Nay,' said he grimly, 'I fear not. She hath lost already what is more than life; and she shall have air enough soon. To-morrow the ship is ready, and we return to England. None knoweth of our stain here, not one, and if the town hath a child unaccounted for to rear in decent ways — why, it is not the first, even here. It will be well enough cared for! And truly we have matter for thankfulness, that her cousin is yet willing to marry her.'

'Hast thou told him?'

'Aye! Thinkest thou I would cast shame into another man's house, unknowing it? He hath always desired her, but she would none of him, the stubborn! She hath small choice now!'

'Will he be kind, Samuel? Can he — '

'Kind? What call'st thou it to take such as she to wife? Kind! How many men would take her, an' she had double the fortune? And being of the family already, he is glad to hide the blot forever.'

'An' if she would not? He is but a coarse fellow, and she ever shunned him.'

'Art thou mad, woman? She weddeth him ere we sail tomorrow, or she stayeth ever in that chamber. The girl is not so sheer a fool! He maketh an honest woman of her, and saveth our house from open shame. What other hope for her than a new life to cover the old? Let her have an honest child, an' she so longeth for one!'

He strode heavily across the porch, till the loose planks creaked again, strode back and forth, with his arms folded and his brows fiercely knit above his iron mouth.

Overhead the shadows flickered mockingly

across a white face among the leaves, with eyes of wasted fire.

* * *

'O, George, what a house! What a lovely house! I am sure it's haunted! Let us get that house to live in this summer! We will have Kate and Jack and Susy and Jim of course, and a splendid time of it!'

Young husbands are indulgent, but still they have to recognize facts.

'My dear, the house may not be to rent; and it may also not be habitable.'

'There is surely somebody in it. I am going to inquire!'

The great central gate was rusted off its hinges, and the long drive had trees in it, but a little footpath showed signs of steady usage, and up that Mrs Jenny went, followed by her obedient George. The front windows of the old mansion were blank, but in a wing at the back they found white curtains and open doors. Outside, in the clear May sunshine, a woman was washing. She was polite and friendly, and evidently glad of visitors in that lonely place. She 'guessed it could be rented — didn't know.' The heirs were in Europe, but 'there was a lawyer in New York had the lettin' of it.' There had been folks there years

70

ago, but not in her time. She and her husband had the rent of their part for taking care of the place. 'Not that they took much care on't either, but keepin' robbers out.' It was furnished throughout, old-fashioned enough, but good; and if they took it she could do the work for 'em herself, she guessed — 'if *he* was willin'!'

Never was a crazy scheme more easily arranged. George knew that lawyer in New York; the rent was not alarming; and the nearness to a rising sea-shore resort made it a still pleasanter place to spend the summer.

Kate and Jack and Susy and Jim cheerfully accepted, and the June moon found them all sitting on the high front porch.

They had explored the house from top to bottom, from the great room in the garret, with nothing in it but a rickety cradle, to the well in the cellar without a curb and with a rusty chain going down to unknown blackness below. They had explored the grounds, once beautiful with rare trees and shrubs, but now a gloomy wilderness of tangled shade.

The old lilacs and laburnums, the spirea and syringa, nodded against the second-story windows. What garden plants survived were great ragged bushes or great shapeless beds. A huge wistaria vine covered the whole front of the house. The trunk, it was too large to call a stem, rose at the corner of the porch by the high steps, and had once climbed its pillars; but now the pillars were wrenched from their places and held rigid and helpless by the tightly wound and knotted arms.

It fenced in all the upper story of the porch with a knitted wall of stem and leaf; it ran along the eaves, holding up the gutter that had once supported it; it shaded every window with heavy green; and the drooping, fragrant blossoms made a waving sheet of purple from roof to ground.

'Did you ever see such a wistaria!' cried ecstatic Mrs Jenny. 'It is worth the rent just to sit under such a vine, — a fig tree beside it would be sheer superfluity and wicked extravagance!'

'Jenny makes much of her wistaria,' said George, 'because she's so disappointed about the ghosts. She made up her mind at first sight to have ghosts in the house, and she can't find even a ghost story!'

'No,' Jenny assented mournfully; 'I pumped poor Mrs Pepperill for three days, but could get nothing out of her. But I'm convinced there is a story, if we could only find it. You need not tell me that a house like this, with a garden like this, and a cellar like this, isn't haunted!'

'I agree with you,' said Jack. Jack was a

reporter on a New York daily, and engaged to Mrs Jenny's pretty sister. 'And if we don't find a real ghost, you may be very sure I shall make one. It's too good an opportunity to lose!'

The pretty sister, who sat next him, resented. 'You shan't do anything of the sort, Jack! This is a *real* ghostly place, and I won't have you make fun of it! Look at that group of trees out there in the long grass — it looks for all the world like a crouching, hunted figure!'

'It looks to me like a woman picking huckleberries,' said Jim, who was married to George's pretty sister.

'Be still, Jim!' said that fair young woman. 'I believe in Jenny's ghost as much as she does. Such a place! Just look at this great wistaria trunk crawling up by the steps here! It looks for all the world like a writhing body — cringing — beseeching!'

'Yes,' answered the subdued Jim, 'it does, Susy. See its waist, — about two yards of it, and twisted at that! A waste of good material!'

'Don't be so horrid, boys! Go off and smoke somewhere if you can't be congenial!'

'We can! We will! We'll be as ghostly as you please.' And forthwith they began to see bloodstains and crouching figures so plentifully that the most delightful shivers multiplied, and the fair enthusiasts started for bed, declaring they should never sleep a wink.

'We shall all surely dream,' cried Mrs Jenny, 'and we must all tell our dreams in the morning!'

'There's another thing certain,' said George, catching Susy as she tripped over a loose plank; 'and that is that you frisky creatures must use the side door till I get this Eiffel tower of a portico fixed, or we shall have some fresh ghosts on our hands! We found a plank here that yawns like a trap-door — big enough to swallow you, — and I believe the bottom of the thing is in China!'

The next morning found them all alive, and eating a substantial New England breakfast, to the accompaniment of saws and hammers on the porch, where carpenters of quite miraculous promptness were tearing things to pieces generally.

'It's got to come down mostly,' they had said. 'These timbers are clean rotted through, what ain't pulled out o' line by this great creeper. That's about all that holds the thing up.'

There was clear reason in what they said, and with a caution from anxious Mrs Jenny not to hurt the wistaria, they were left to demolish and repair at leisure.

'How about ghosts?' asked Jack after a fourth griddle cake. 'I had one, and it's taken away my appetite!'

Mrs Jenny gave a little shriek and dropped her knife and fork.

'Oh, so had I! I had the most awful — well, not dream exactly, but feeling. I had forgotten all about it!'

'Must have been awful,' said Jack, taking another cake. 'Do tell us about the feeling. My ghost will wait.'

'It makes me creep to think of it even now,' she said. 'I woke up, all at once, with that dreadful feeling as if something were going to happen, you know! I was wide awake, and hearing every little sound for miles around, it seemed to me. There are so many strange little noises in the country for all it is so still. Millions of crickets and things outside, and all kinds of rustles in the trees! There wasn't much wind, and the moonlight came through in my three great windows in three white squares on the black old floor, and those fingery wistaria leaves we were talking of last night just seemed to crawl all over them. And — O, girls, you know that dreadful well in the cellar?'

A most gratifying impression was made by this, and Jenny proceeded cheerfully:

'Well, while it was so horridly still, and I lay

there trying not to wake George, I heard as plainly as if it were right in the room, that old chain down there rattle and creak over the stones!'

'Bravo!' cried Jack. 'That's fine! I'll put it in the Sunday edition!'

'Be still!' said Kate. 'What was it, Jenny? Did you really see anything?'

'No, I didn't, I'm sorry to say. But just then I didn't want to. I woke George, and made such a fuss that he gave me bromide, and said he'd go and look, and that's the last I thought of it till Jack reminded me, — the bromide worked so well.'

'Now, Jack, give us yours,' said Jim. 'Maybe, it will dovetail in somehow. Thirsty ghost, I imagine; maybe they had prohibition here even then!'

Jack folded his napkin, and leaned back in his most impressive manner.

'It was striking twelve by the great hall clock — ' he began.

'There isn't any hall clock!'

'O hush, Jim, you spoil the current! It was just one o'clock then, by my old-fashioned repeater.'

'Waterbury! Never mind what time it was!'

'Well, honestly, I woke up sharp, like our beloved hostess, and tried to go to sleep again, but couldn't. I experienced all those moonlight and grasshopper sensations, just like Jenny, and was wondering what could have been the matter with the supper, when in came my ghost, and I knew it was all a dream! It was a female ghost, and I imagine she was young and handsome, but all those crouching, hunted figures of last evening ran riot in my brain, and this poor creature looked just like them. She was all wrapped up in a shawl, and had a big bundle under her arm, — dear me, I am spoiling the story! With the air and gait of one in frantic haste and terror, the muffled figure glided to a dark old bureau, and seemed taking things from the drawers. As she turned, the moonlight shone full on a little red cross that hung from her neck by a thin gold chain — I saw it glitter as she crept noiselessly from the room! That's all.'

'O Jack, don't be so horrid! Did you really? Is that all! What do you think it was?'

'I am not horrid by nature, only professionally. I really did. That was all. And I am fully convinced it was the genuine, legitimate ghost of an eloping chambermaid with klepto-mania!'

'You are too bad, Jack!' cried Jenny. 'You take all the horror out of it. There isn't a 'creep' left among us.'

'It's no time for creeps at nine-thirty a.m.,

with sunlight and carpenters outside! However, if you can't wait till twilight for your creeps, I think I can furnish one or two,' said George. 'I went down cellar after Jenny's ghost!'

There was a delighted chorus of female voices, and Jenny cast upon her lord a glance of genuine gratitude.

'It's all very well to lie in bed and see ghosts, or hear them,' he went on. 'But the young householder suspecteth burglars, even though as a medical man he knoweth nerves, and after Jenny dropped off I started on a voyage of discovery. I never will again, I promise you!'

'Why, what *was* it?'

'Oh, George!'

'I got a candle — '

'Good mark for the burglars,' murmured Jack.

'And went all over the house, gradually working down to the cellar and the well.'

'Well?' said Jack.

'Now you can laugh; but that cellar is no joke by daylight, and a candle there at night is about as inspiring as a lightning-bug in the Mammoth Cave. I went along with the light, trying not to fall into the well prematurely; got to it all at once; held the light down and *then* I saw, right under my feet — (I nearly fell over her, or walked through her, perhaps),

— a woman, hunched up under a shawl! She had hold of the chain, and the candle shone on her hands — white, thin hands, — on a little red cross that hung from her neck — *vide* Jack! I'm no believer in ghosts, and I firmly object to unknown parties in the house at night; so I spoke to her rather fiercely. She didn't seem to notice that, and I reached down to take hold of her, — then I came upstairs!'

'What for?'

'What happened?'

'What was the matter?'

'Well, nothing happened. Only she wasn't there! May have been indigestion, of course, but as a physician I don't advise any one to court indigestion alone at midnight in a cellar!'

'This is the most interesting and peripatetic and evasive ghost I ever heard of!' said Jack. 'It's my belief she has no end of silver tankards, and jewels galore, at the bottom of that well, and I move we go and see!'

'To the bottom of the well, Jack?'

'To the bottom of the mystery. Come on!'

There was unanimous assent, and the fresh cambrics and pretty boots were gallantly escorted below by gentlemen whose jokes were so frequent that many of them were a little forced.

The deep old cellar was so dark that they had to bring lights, and the well so gloomy in its blackness that the ladies recoiled.

'That well is enough to scare even a ghost. It's my opinion you'd better let well enough alone?' quoth Jim.

'Truth lies hid in a well, and we must get her out,' said George. 'Bear a hand with the chain?'

Jim pulled away on the chain, George turned the creaking windlass, and Jack was chorus.

'A wet sheet for this ghost, if not a flowing sea,' said he. 'Seems to be hard work raising spirits! I suppose he kicked the bucket when he went down!'

As the chain lightened and shortened there grew a strained silence among them; and when at length the bucket appeared, rising slowly through the dark water, there was an eager, half reluctant peering, and a natural drawing back. They poked the gloomy contents. 'Only water.'

'Nothing but mud.'

'Something — '

They emptied the bucket up on the dark earth, and then the girls all went out into the air, into the bright warm sunshine in front of the house, where was the sound of saw and hammer, and the smell of new wood. There was nothing said until the men joined them, and then Jenny timidly asked:

'How old should you think it was, George?'

'All of a century,' he answered. 'That water is a preservative, — lime in it. Oh! — you mean? — Not more than a month; a very little baby!'

There was another silence at this, broken by a cry from the workmen. They had removed the floor and the side walls of the old porch, so that the sunshine poured down to the dark stones of the cellar bottom. And there, in the strangling grasp of the roots of the great wistaria, lay the bones of a woman, from whose neck still hung a tiny scarlet cross on a thin chain of gold.

Through This

The dawn colors creep up my bedroom wall, softly, slowly.

Darkness, dim gray, dull blue, soft lavender, clear pink, pale yellow, warm gold — sunlight.

A new day.

With the great sunrise great thoughts come.

I rise with the world. I live, I can help. Here close at hand lie the sweet home duties through which my life shall touch the others! Through this man made happier and stronger by my living; through these rosy babies sleeping here in the growing light; through this small, sweet, well-ordered home, whose restful influence shall touch all comers; through me too, perhaps — there's the baker, I must get up, or this bright purpose fades.

How well the fire burns! Its swift kindling and gathering roar speak of accomplishment. The rich odor of coffee steals through the house.

John likes morning-glories on the breakfast table — scented flowers are better with lighter meals. All is ready — healthful, dainty, delicious.

The clean-aproned little ones smile milky-mouthed over their bowls of mush. John kisses me good-bye so happily.

Through this dear work, well done, I shall reach, I shall help — but I must get the dishes done and not dream.

'Good morning! Soap, please, the same kind. Coffee, rice, two boxes of gelatine. That's all, I think. Oh — crackers! Good morning.'

There, I forgot the eggs! I can make these go, I guess. Now to soak the tapioca. Now the beets on, they take so long. I'll bake the potatoes — they don't go in yet. Now babykins must have her bath and nap.

A clean hour and a half before dinner. I can get those little nightgowns cut and basted. How bright the sun is! Amaranth lies on the grass under the rosebush, stretching her paws among the warm, green blades. The kittens tumble over her. She's brought them three mice this week. Baby and Jack are on the warm grass too — happy, safe, well. Careful, dear! Don't go away from little sister!

By and by when they are grown, I can — O there! The bell!

Ah, well! — Yes — I'd like to have joined. I believe in it, but I can't now. Home duties forbid. This is my work. Through this, in time — there's the bell again, and it waked the baby!

As if I could buy a sewing machine every week! I'll put out a bulletin, stating my needs for the benefit of agents. I don't believe in buying at the door anyway, yet I suppose they must live. Yes, dear! Mamma's coming!

I wonder if torchon would look better, or Hamburg? It's softer but it looks older. Oh, here's that knit edging grandma sent me. Bless her dear heart!

There! I meant to have swept the bed-room this morning so as to have more time to-morrow. Perhaps I can before dinner. It does look dreadfully. I'll just put the potatoes in. Baked potatoes are so good! I love to see Jack dig into them with his little spoon.

John says I cook steak better than anyone he ever saw.

Yes, dear?

Is that so? Why, I should think they'd *know* better. Can't the people do anything about it?

Why no — not *personally* — but I should think *you* might. What are men for if they can't keep the city in order.

Cream on the pudding, dear?

That was a good dinner. I like to cook. I think housework is noble if you do it in a right spirit.

That pipe must be seen to before long. I'll speak to John about it. Coal's pretty low, too.

Guess I'll put on my best boots, I want to

run down town for a few moments — in case mother comes and can stay with baby. I wonder if mother wouldn't like to join that — she has time enough. But she doesn't seem a bit interested in outside things. I ought to take baby out in her carriage, but it's so heavy with Jack, and yet Jack can't walk a great way. Besides, if mother comes I needn't. Maybe we'll all go in the car — but that's such an undertaking! Three o'clock!

Jack! Jack! Don't do that — here — wait a moment.

I ought to answer Jennie's letter. She writes such splendid things, but I don't go with her in half she says. A woman cannot do that way and keep a family going. I'll write to her this evening.

Of course, if one *could*, I'd like as well as anyone to be in those great live currents of thought and action. Jennie and I were full of it in school. How long ago that seems. But I never thought then of being so happy. Jennie isn't happy, I know — she can't be, poor thing, till she's a wife and mother.

O, there comes mother! Jack, deary, open the gate for Grandma! So glad you could come, mother dear! Can you stay awhile and let me go down town on a few errands?

Mother looks real tired. I wish she would go out more and have some outside interests.

Mary and the children are too much for her, I think. Harry ought not to have brought them home. Mother needs rest. She's brought up one family.

There, I've forgotten my list, I hurried so. Thread, elastic, buttons; what was that other thing? Maybe I'll think of it.

How awfully cheap! How can they make them at that price! Three, please. I guess with these I can make the others last through the year. They're so pretty, too. How much are these? Jack's got to have a new coat before long — not to-day.

O, dear! I've missed that car, and mother can't stay after five! I'll cut across and hurry.

Why, the milk hasn't come, and John's got to go out early tonight. I wish election was over.

I'm sorry, dear, but the milk was so late I couldn't make it. Yes, I'll speak to him. O, no, I guess not; he's a very reliable man, usually, and the milk's good. Hush, hush, baby! Papa's talking!

Good night, dear, don't be too late.

Sleep, baby, sleep!
The large stars are the sheep,
The little stars are the lambs, I guess,
And the fair moon is the shepherdess.
Sleep, baby, sleep!

89

How pretty they look. Thank God, they keep so well.

It's no use, I can't write a letter to-night — especially to Jennie. I'm too tired. I'll go to bed early. John hates to have me wait up for him late. I'll go now, if it is before dark — then get up early tomorrow and get the sweeping done. How loud the crickets are! The evening shades creep down my bedroom wall — softly — slowly.

Warm gold — pale yellow — clear pink — soft lavender — dull blue — dim gray-darkness.

An Extinct Angel

There was once a species of angel inhabiting this planet, acting as 'a universal solvent' to all the jarring, irreconcilable elements of human life.

It was quite numerous; almost every family had one; and, although differing in degree of seraphic virtue, all were, by common consent, angels.

The advantages of possessing such a creature were untold. In the first place, the chances of the mere human being in the way of getting to heaven were greatly increased by these semi-heavenly belongings; they gave one a sort of lien on the next world, a practical claim most comforting to the owner.

For the angels of course possessed virtues above mere humanity; and because the angels were so well-behaved, therefore the owners were given credit.

Beside this direct advantage of complimentary tickets up above were innumerable indirect advantages below. The possession of one of these angels smoothed every feature of life, and gave peace and joy to an otherwise hard lot.

It was the business of the angel to assuage,

to soothe, to comfort, to delight. No matter how unruly were the passions of the owner, sometimes even to the extent of legally beating his angel with 'a stick no thicker than his thumb,' the angel was to have no passion whatever — unless self-sacrifice may be called a passion, and indeed it often amounted to one with her.

The human creature went out to his daily toil and comforted himself as he saw fit. He was apt to come home tired and cross, and in this exigency it was the business of the angel to wear a smile for his benefit — a soft, perennial, heavenly smile.

By an unfortunate limitation of humanity the angel was required, in addition to such celestial duties as smiling and soothing, to do kitchen service, cleaning, sewing, nursing, and other mundane tasks. But these things must be accomplished without the slightest diminution of the angelic virtues.

The angelic virtues, by the way, were of a curiously paradoxical nature.

They were inherent. A human being did not pretend to name them, could not be expected to have them, acknowledged them as far beyond his gross earthly nature; and yet, for all this, he kept constant watch over the virtues of the angel, wrote whole books of advice for angels on how they should behave, and openly held that angels would lose their virtues altogether should they once cease to obey the will and defer to the judgment of human kind.

This looks strange to us to-day as we consider these past conditions, but then it seemed fair enough; and the angels — bless their submissive, patient hearts! — never thought of questioning it.

It was perhaps only to be expected that when an angel fell the human creature should punish the celestial creature with unrelenting fury. It was so much easier to be an angel than to be human, that there was no excuse for an angel's falling, even by means of her own angelic pity and tender affection.

It seems perhaps hard that the very human creature the angel fell on, or fell with, or fell to — however you choose to put it — was as harsh as anyone in condemnation of the fall. He never assisted the angel to rise, but got out from under and resumed his way, leaving her in the mud. She was a great convenience to walk on, and, as was stoutly maintained by the human creature, helped keep the other angels clean.

This is exceedingly mysterious, and had better not be inquired into too closely.

The amount of physical labor of a severe and degrading sort required of one of these bright spirits, was amazing. Certain kinds of work — always and essentially dirty — were relegated wholly to her. Yet one of her first and most rigid duties was the keeping of her angelic robes spotlessly clean.

The human creature took great delight in contemplating the flowing robes of the angels. Their changeful motion suggested to him all manner of sweet and lovely thoughts and memories; also, the angelic virtues above mentioned were supposed largely to inhere in the flowing robes. Therefore flow they must, and the ample garments waved unchecked over the weary limbs of the wearer, the contiguous furniture and the stairs. For the angels unfortunately had no wings, and their work was such as required a good deal of going up and down stairs.

It is quite a peculiar thing, in contemplating this work, to see how largely it consisted in dealing with dirt. Yes, it does seem strange to this enlightened age; but the fact was that the angels waited on the human creatures in every form of menial service, doing things as their natural duty which the human creature loathed and scorned.

It does seem irreconcilable, but they reconciled it. The angel was an angel and the work was the angel's work, and what more do you want?

There is one thing about the subject which looks a little suspicious: The angels — I say it under breath — were not very bright!

The human creatures did not like intelligent angels — intelligence seemed to dim their shine, somehow, and pale their virtues. It was harder to reconcile things where the angels had any sense. Therefore every possible care was taken to prevent the angels from learning anything of our gross human wisdom.

But little by little, owing to the unthought-of consequences of repeated intermarriage between the angel and the human being, the angel longed for, found and ate the fruit of the forbidden tree of knowledge.

And in that day she surely died.

The species is now extinct. It is rumored that here and there in remote regions you can still find a solitary specimen — in places where no access is to be had to the deadly fruit; but the race as a race is extinct.

Poor dodo!

The Unexpected

I

'It is the unexpected which happens,' says the French proverb. I like the proverb, because it is true — and because it is French.

Edouard Charpentier is my name.

I am an American by birth, but that is all. From infancy, when I had a French nurse; in childhood, when I had a French governess; through youth, passed in a French school; to manhood, devoted to French art, I have been French by sympathy and education.

France — modern France — and French art — modern French art — I adore!

My school is the 'pleine-aire,' and my master, could I but find him, is M. Duchesne. M. Duchesne has had pictures in the Salon for three years, and pictures elsewhere, eagerly bought, and yet Paris knows not M. Duchesne. We know his house, his horse, his carriage, his servants and his garden-wall, but he sees no one, speaks to no one; indeed, he has left Paris for a time, and we worship afar off.

I have a sketch by this master which I

treasure jealously — a pencil sketch of a great picture yet to come. I await it.

M. Duchesne paints from the model, and I paint from the model, exclusively. It is the only way to be firm, accurate, true. Without the model we may have German fantasy or English domesticity, but no modern French art.

It is hard, too, to get models continually when one is but a student after five years' work, and one's pictures bring francs indeed, but not dollars.

Still, there is Georgette!

There, also, were Emilie and Pauline. But now it is Georgette, and she is adorable!

'Tis true, she has not much soul; but, then, she has a charming body, and 'tis that I copy.

Georgette and I get on together to admiration. How much better is this than matrimony for an artist! How wise is M. Daudet!

Antoine is my dearest friend. I paint with him, and we are happy. Georgette is my dearest model. I paint from her, and we are happy.

Into this peaceful scene comes a letter from America, bringing much emotion.

It appears I had a great-uncle there, in some northeastern corner of New England. Maine? No; Vermont.

And it appears, strangely enough, that this northeastern great-uncle was seized in his old age with a passion for French art; at least I know not how else to account for his hunting me up through a lawyer and leaving me some quarter of a million when he died.

An admirable great-uncle!

But I must go home and settle the property; that is imperative. I must leave Paris, I must leave Antoine, I must leave Georgette!

Could anything be further from Paris than a town in Vermont? No, not the Andaman Islands.

And could anything be further from Antoine and Georgette than the family of great-cousins I find myself among?

But one of them — ah, Heaven! some forty-seventh cousin who is so beautiful that I forget she is an American, I forget Paris, I forget Antoine — yes, and even Georgette! Poor Georgette! But this is fate.

This cousin is not like the other cousins. I pursue, I inquire, I ascertain.

Her name is Mary D. Greenleaf. I shall call her Marie.

And she comes from Boston.

But, beyond the name, how can I describe her? I have seen beauty, yes, much beauty, in maid, matron and model, but I never saw anything to equal this country girl. What a figure!

No, not a 'figure' — the word shames her.

She has a body, the body of a young Diana, and a body and a figure are two very different things. I am an artist, and I have lived in Paris, and I know the difference.

The lawyers in Boston can settle that property, I find.

The air is delightful in northern Vermont in March. There are mountains, clouds, trees. I will paint here a while. Ah, yes; and I will assist this shy young soul!

'Cousin Marie,' say I, 'come, let me teach you to paint!'

'It would be too difficult for you, Mr Carpenter — it would take too long!'

'Call me Edouard!' I cry. 'Are we not cousins? Cousin Edouard, I beg of you! And nothing is difficult when you are with me, Marie — nothing can be too long at your side!'

'Thanks, cousin Edward, but I think I will not impose on your good nature. Besides, I shall not stay here. I go back to Boston, to my aunt.'

I find the air of Boston is good in March, and there are places of interest there, and rising American artists who deserve encouragement. I will stay in Boston a while to assist the lawyers in settling my property; it is necessary.

I visit Marie continually. Am I not a cousin? I talk to her of life, of art, of Paris, of M.

Duchesne. I show her my precious sketch.

'But,' says she, 'I am not wholly a wood nymph, as you seem fondly to imagine. I have been to Paris myself — with my uncle — years since.'

'Fairest cousin,' say I, 'if you had not been even to Boston, I should still love you! Come and see Paris again — with me!' And then she would laugh at me and send me away. Ah, yes! I had come even to marriage, you see!

I soon found she had the usual woman's faith in those conventions. I gave her 'Artists' Wives.' She said she had read it. She laughed at Daudet and me!

I talked to her of ruined geniuses I had known myself, but she said a ruined genius was no worse than a ruined woman! One cannot reason with young girls!

Do not believe I succumbed without a struggle. I even tore myself away and went to New York. It was not far enough, I fear. I soon came back.

She lived with an aunt — my adorable little precisian! — with a horrible strong-minded aunt, and such a life as I led between them for a whole month!

I call continually. I bury her in flowers. I take her to the theatre, aunt and all. And at this the aunt seemed greatly surprised, but I disapprove of American familiarities. No; my wife — and wife she must be — shall be treated with punctilious respect.

Never was I so laughed at and argued with in my life as I was laughed at by that dreadful beauty, and argued with by that dreadful aunt.

The only rest was in pictures. Marie would look at pictures always, and seemed to have a real appreciation of them, almost an understanding, of a sort. So that I began to hope — dimly and faintly to hope — that she might grow to care for mine. To have a wife who would care for one's art, who would come to one's studio — but, then, the models! I paint from the model almost entirely, as I said, and I know what women are about models, without Daudet to tell me!

And this prudish New England girl! Well, she might come to the studio on stated days, and perhaps in time I might lead her gently to understand.

That I should ever live to commit matrimony! But Fate rules all men.

I think that girl refused me nine times. She always put me off with absurd excuses and reasons: said I didn't know her yet; said we should never agree; said I was French and she was American; said I cared more for art than I did for her! At that I earnestly assured her that I would become an organ-grinder or a bank-clerk rather than lose her — and then she seemed downright angry, and sent me away again.

Women are strangely inconsistent!

She always sent me away, but I always came back.

After about a month of this torture, I chanced to find her, one soft May twilight, without the aunt, sitting by a window in the fragrant dusk.

She had flowers in her hand — flowers I had sent her — and sat looking down at them, her strong, pure profile clear against the saffron sky.

I came in quietly, and stood watching, in a rapture of hope and admiration. And while I watched I saw a great pearl tear roll down among my violets.

That was enough.

I sprang forward, I knelt beside her, I caught her hands in mine, I drew her to me, I cried, exultantly: 'You love me! And I — ah, God! How I love you!'

Even then she would have put me from her. She insisted that I did not know her yet, that she ought to tell me — but I held her close and kissed away her words, and said: 'You love me, perfect one, and I love you. The rest will be right.'

Then she laid her white hands on my shoulders, and looked deep into my eyes.

'I believe that is true,' said she; 'and I will marry you, Edward.'

She dropped her face on my shoulder then — that face of fire and roses — and we were still.

II

It is but two months' time from then; I have been married a fortnight. The first week was heaven — and the second was hell! O my God! My wife! That young Diana to be but — ! I have borne it a week. I have feared and despised myself. I have suspected and hated myself. I have discovered and cursed myself. Aye, and cursed her, and *him,* whom this day I shall kill!

It is now three o'clock. I cannot kill him until four, for he comes not till then.

I am very comfortable here in this room opposite — very comfortable; and I can wait and think and remember.

Let me think.

First, to kill him. That is simple and easily settled.

Shall I kill her?

If she lived, could I ever see her again? Ever touch that hand — those lips — that, within two weeks of marriage — ? No, she shall die!

And, if she lived, what would be before her but more shame, and more, till she felt it herself?

Far better that she die!

And I?

Could I live to forget her? To carry always in my heart a black stone across that door? To rise and rise, and do great work — *alone!*

Never! I cannot forget her!

Better die with her, even now.

Hark! Is that a step on the stair? Not yet.

My money is well bestowed. Antoine is a better artist than I, and a better man, and the money will widen and lighten a noble life in his hands.

And little Georgette is provided for. How long ago, how faint and weak, that seems! But Georgette loved me, I believe, at least for a time — longer than a week.

To wait — until four o'clock!

To think — I have thought; it is all arranged!

These pistols, that she admired but day before yesterday, that we practised with together, both loaded full. What a shot she is! I believe she can do everything!

To wait — to think — to remember.

Let me remember.

I knew her a week, wooed her a month, have been married a fortnight.

She always said I didn't know her. She was always on the point of telling me something, and I would not let her. She seemed half repentant, half in jest — I preferred to trust her. Those clear, brown eyes — clear and bright, like brook water with the sun through it! And she would smile so! 'Tis not that I must remember.

Am I sure? Sure! I laugh at myself.

What would you call it, you — any man? A young woman steals from her house, alone, every day, and comes privately, cloaked and veiled, to this place, this den of Bohemians, this building of New York studios! Painters? I know them — I am a painter myself.

She goes to this room, day after day, and tells me nothing.

I say to her gently: 'What do you do with your days, my love?'

'Oh, many things,' she answers; 'I am studying art — to please you!'

That was ingenious. She knew she might be watched.

I say, 'Cannot I teach you?' and she says, 'I have a teacher I used to study with. I must finish. I want to surprise you!' So she would soothe me — to appearance.

But I watch and follow, I take this little room. I wait, and I see.

Lessons? Oh, perjured one! There is no

tenant of that room but yourself, and to it *he* comes each day.

Is that a step? Not yet. I watch and wait. This is America, I say, not France. This is my wife. I will trust her. But the man comes every day. He is young. He is handsome — handsome as a fiend.

I cannot bear it. I go to the door. I knock. There is no response. I try the door. It is locked. I stoop and look through the key-hole. What do I see? Ah, God! The hat and cloak of that man upon a chair, and then only a tall screen. Behind that screen, low voices!

I did not go home last night. I am here to-day — with these!

That is a step. Yes! Softly, now. He has gone in. I heard her speak. She said: 'You are late, Guillaume!'

Let me give them a little time.

Now — softly — I come, friends. *I* am not late!

III

Across the narrow passage I steal, noiselessly. The door is unlocked this time. I burst in.

There stands my young wife, pale, trembling, startled, unable to speak.

There is the handsome Guillaume — behind

the screen. My fingers press the triggers. There is a sharp double report. Guillaume tumbles over, howling, and Marie flings herself between us.

'Edward! One moment! Give me a moment for my life! The pistols are harmless, dear — blank cartridges. I fixed them myself. I saw you suspected. But you've spoiled my surprise. I shall have to tell you now. This is my studio, love. Here is the picture you have the sketch of. *I* am 'M. Duchesne' — Mary Duchesne Greenleaf Carpenter — and this is my model!'

IV

We are very happy in Paris, with our double studio. We sometimes share our models. We laugh at M. Daudet.

Making a Change

'Wa-a-a-a! Waa-a-a-aaa!'

Frank Gordins set down his coffee cup so hard that it spilled over into the saucer.

'Is there no way to stop that child crying?' he demanded.

'I do not know of any,' said his wife, so definitely and politely that the words seemed cut off by machinery.

'*I do*,' said his mother with even more definiteness, but less politeness.

Young Mrs Gordins looked at her mother-in-law from under her delicate level brows, and said nothing. But the weary lines about her eyes deepened; she had been kept awake nearly all night, and for many nights.

So had he. So, as a matter of fact, had his mother. She had not the care of the baby — but lay awake wishing she had.

'There's no need at all for that child's crying so, Frank. If Julia would only let me — '

'It's no use talking about it,' said Julia. 'If Frank is not satisfied with the child's mother he must say so — perhaps we can make a change.'

This was ominously gentle. Julia's nerves were at the breaking point. Upon her tired ears, her sensitive mother's heart, the grating wail from the next room fell like a lash — burnt in like fire. Her ears were hypersensitive, always. She had been an ardent musician before her marriage, and had taught quite successfully on both piano and violin. To any mother a child's cry is painful; to a musical mother it is torment.

But if her ears were sensitive, so was her conscience. If her nerves were weak her pride was strong. The child was her child, it was her duty to take care of it, and take care of it she would. She spent her days in unremitting devotion to its needs, and to the care of her neat flat; and her nights had long since ceased to refresh her.

Again the weary cry rose to a wail.

'It does seem to be time for a change of treatment,' suggested the older woman acidly.

'Or a change of residence,' offered the younger, in a deadly quiet voice.

'Well, by Jupiter! There'll be a change of some kind, and p. d. q.!' said the son and husband, rising to his feet.

His mother rose also, and left the room, holding her head high and refusing to show any effects of that last thrust.

Frank Gordins glared at his wife. His

nerves were raw, too. It does not benefit any one in health or character to be continuously deprived of sleep. Some enlightened persons use that deprivation as a form of torture.

She stirred her coffee with mechanical calm, her eyes sullenly bent on her plate.

'I will not stand having Mother spoken to like that,' he stated with decision.

'I will not stand having her interfere with my methods of bringing up children.'

'Your methods! Why, Julia, my mother knows more about taking care of babies than you'll ever learn! She has the real love of it — and the practical experience. Why can't you *let* her take care of the kid — and we'll all have some peace!'

She lifted her eyes and looked at him; deep inscrutable wells of angry light. He had not the faintest appreciation of her state of mind. When people say they are 'nearly crazy' from weariness, they state a practical fact. The old phrase which describes reason as 'tottering on her throne,' is also a clear one.

Julia was more near the verge of complete disaster than the family dreamed. The conditions were so simple, so usual, so inevitable.

Here was Frank Gordins, well brought up, the only son of a very capable and idolatrously affectionate mother. He had fallen deeply and desperately in love with the exalted beauty and fine mind of the young music teacher, and his mother had approved. She too loved music and admired beauty.

Her tiny store in the savings bank did not allow of a separate home, and Julia had cordially welcomed her to share in their household.

Here was affection, propriety and peace. Here was a noble devotion on the part of the young wife, who so worshipped her husband that she used to wish she had been the greatest musician on earth — that she might give it up for him! She had given up her music, perforce, for many months, and missed it more than she knew.

She bent her mind to the decoration and artistic management of their little apartment, finding her standards difficult to maintain by the ever-changing inefficiency of her help. The musical temperament does not always include patience; nor, necessarily, the power of management.

When the baby came her heart overflowed with utter devotion and thankfulness; she was his wife — the mother of his child. Her happiness lifted and pushed within till she longed more than ever for her music for the free pouring current of expression, to give forth her love and pride and happiness. She had not the gift of words.

So now she looked at her husband, dumbly, while wild visions of separation, of secret flight — even of self-destruction — swung dizzily across her mental vision. All she said was 'All right, Frank. We'll make a change. And you shall have — some peace.'

'Thank goodness for that, Jule! You do look tired, Girlie — let Mother see to His Nibs, and try to get a nap, can't you?'

'Yes,' she said. 'Yes . . . I think I will.' Her voice had a peculiar note in it. If Frank had been an alienist, or even a general physician, he would have noticed it. But his work lay in electric coils, in dynamos and copper wiring — not in woman's nerves — and he did not notice it.

He kissed her and went out, throwing back his shoulders and drawing a long breath of relief as he left the house behind him and entered his own world.

'This being married — and bringing up children — is not what it's cracked up to be.' That was the feeling in the back of his mind. But it did not find full admission, much less expression.

When a friend asked him, 'All well at home?' he said, 'Yes, thank you — pretty fair. Kid cries a good deal — but that's natural, I suppose.'

He dismissed the whole matter from his

mind and bent his faculties to a man's task — how he can earn enough to support a wife, a mother, and a son.

At home his mother sat in her small room, looking out of the window at the ground glass one just across the 'well,' and thinking hard.

By the disorderly little breakfast table his wife remained motionless, her chin in her hands, her big eyes staring at nothing, trying to formulate in her weary mind some reliable reason why she should not do what she was thinking of doing. But her mind was too exhausted to serve her properly.

Sleep — Sleep — Sleep — that was the one thing she wanted. Then his mother could take care of the baby all she wanted to, and Frank could have some peace . . . Oh, dear! It was time for the child's bath.

She gave it to him mechanically. On the stroke of the hour she prepared the sterilized milk, and arranged the little one comfortably with his bottle. He snuggled down, enjoying it, while she stood watching him.

She emptied the tub, put the bath apron to dry, picked up all the towels and sponges and varied appurtenances of the elaborate performance of bathing the first-born, and then sat staring straight before her, more weary than ever, but growing inwardly determined.

Greta had cleared the table, with heavy

heels and hands, and was now rattling dishes in the kitchen. At every slam the young mother winced, and when the girl's high voice began a sort of doleful chant over her work, young Mrs Gordins rose to her feet with a shiver, and made her decision.

She carefully picked up the child and his bottle, and carried him to his grandmother's room.

'Would you mind looking after Albert?' she asked in a flat, quiet voice; 'I think I'll try to get some sleep.'

'Oh, I shall be delighted,' replied her mother-in-law. She said it in a tone of cold politeness, but Julia did not notice. She laid the child on the bed and stood looking at him in the same dull way for a little while, then went out without another word.

Mrs Gordins, senior, sat watching the baby for some long moments. 'He's a perfectly lovely child!' she said softly, gloating over his rosy beauty. 'There's not a *thing* the matter with him! It's just her absurd ideas. She's so irregular with him! To think of letting that child cry for an hour! He is nervous because she is. And of course she couldn't feed him till after his bath — of course not!'

She continued in these sarcastic meditations for some time, taking the empty bottle away from the small wet mouth, that sucked on for a few moments aimlessly, and then was quiet in sleep.

'I could take care of him so that he'd *never* cry!' she continued to herself, rocking slowly back and forth. 'And I could take care of twenty like him — and enjoy it! I believe I'll go off somewhere and do it. Give Julia a rest. Change of residence, indeed!'

She rocked and planned, pleased to have her grandson with her, even while asleep.

Greta had gone out on some errand of her own. The rooms were very quiet. Suddenly the old lady held up her head and sniffed. She rose swiftly to her feet and sprang to the gas jet — no, it was shut off tightly. She went back to the dining-room — all right there.

'That foolish girl has left the range going and it's blown out!' she thought, and went to the kitchen. No, the little room was fresh and clean; every burner turned off.

'Funny! It must come in from the hall.' She opened the door. No, the hall gave only its usual odor of diffused basement. Then the parlor — nothing there. The little alcove called by the renting agent 'the music room,' where Julia's closed piano and violin case stood dumb and dusty — nothing there.

'It's in her room — and she's asleep!' said Mrs Gordins, senior; and she tried to open the door. It was locked. She knocked —

there was no answer; knocked louder — shook it — rattled the knob. No answer.

Then Mrs Gordins thought quickly. 'It may be an accident, and nobody must know. Frank mustn't know. I'm glad Greta's out. I *must* get in somehow!' She looked at the transom, and the stout rod Frank had himself put up for the portieres Julia loved.

'I believe I can do it, at a pinch.'

She was a remarkably active woman of her years, but no memory of earlier gymnastic feats could quite cover the exercise. She hastily brought the step-ladder. From its top she could see in, and what she saw made her determine recklessly.

Grabbing the pole with small strong hands, she thrust her light frame bravely through the opening, turning clumsily but successfully, and dropping breathlessly and somewhat bruised to the floor, she flew to open the windows and doors.

When Julia opened her eyes she found loving arms around her, and wise, tender words to soothe and reassure.

'Don't say a thing, dearie — I understand. I *understand* I tell you! Oh, my dear girl — my precious daughter! We haven't been half good enough to you, Frank and I! But cheer up now — I've got the *loveliest* plan to tell you about! We *are* going to make a change! Listen now!'

And while the pale young mother lay quiet, petted and waited on to her heart's content, great plans were discussed and decided on.

Frank Gordins was pleased when the baby 'outgrew his crying spells.' He spoke of it to his wife.

'Yes,' she said sweetly. 'He has better care.'

'I knew you'd learn,' said he, proudly.

'I have!' she agreed. 'I've learned — ever so much!'

He was pleased too, vastly pleased, to have her health improve rapidly and steadily, the delicate pink come back to her cheeks, the soft light to her eyes; and when she made music for him in the evening, soft music, with shut doors — not to waken Albert — he felt as if his days of courtship had come again.

Greta the hammer-footed had gone, and an amazing French matron who came in by the day had taken her place. He asked no questions as to this person's peculiarities, and did not know that she did the purchasing and planned the meals, meals of such new delicacy and careful variance as gave him much delight. Neither did he know that her wages were greater than her predecessors. He turned over the same sum weekly, and did not pursue details.

He was pleased also that his mother seemed

to have taken a new lease of life. She was so cheerful and brisk, so full of little jokes and stories — as he had known her in his boyhood; and above all she was so free and affectionate with Julia, that he was more than pleased.

'I tell you what it is!' he said to a bachelor friend. 'You fellows don't know what you're missing!' And he brought one of them home to dinner — just to show him.

'Do you do all that on thirty-five a week?' his friend demanded.

'That's about it,' he answered proudly.

'Well, your wife's a wonderful manager — that's all I can say. And you've got the best cook I ever saw, or heard of, or ate of — I suppose I might say — for five dollars.'

Mr Gordins was pleased and proud. But he was neither pleased nor proud when someone said to him, with displeasing frankness, 'I shouldn't think you'd want your wife to be giving music lessons, Frank!'

He did not show surprise nor anger to his friend, but saved it for his wife. So surprised and so angry was he that he did a most unusual thing — he left his business and went home early in the afternoon. He opened the door of his flat. There was no one in it. He went through every room. No wife; no child; no mother; no servant.

The elevator boy heard him banging about,

opening and shutting doors, and grinned happily. When Mr Gordins came out Charles volunteered some information.

'Young Mrs Gordins is out, Sir; but old Mrs Gordins and the baby — they're upstairs. On the roof, I think.'

Mr Gordins went to the roof. There he found his mother, a smiling, cheerful nurse-maid, and fifteen happy babies.

Mrs Gordins, senior, rose to the occasion promptly.

'Welcome to my baby garden, Frank,' she said cheerfully. 'I'm so glad you could get off in time to see it.'

She took his arm and led him about, proudly exhibiting her sunny roof-garden, her sand-pile, and big, shallow, zinc-lined pool; her flowers and vines, her see-saws, swings, and floor mattresses.

'You see how happy they are,' she said. 'Celia can manage very well for a few moments.' And then she exhibited to him the whole upper flat, turned into a convenient place for many little ones to take their naps or to play in if the weather was bad.

'Where's Julia?' he demanded first.

'Julia will be in presently,' she told him, 'by five o'clock anyway. And the mothers come for the babies by then, too. I have them from nine or ten to five.'

He was silent, both angry and hurt.

'We didn't tell you at first, my dear boy, because we knew you wouldn't like it, and we wanted to make sure it would go well. I rent the upper flat, you see — it is forty dollars a month, same as ours — and pay Celia five dollars a week, and pay Dr Holbrook downstairs the same for looking over my little ones every day. She helped me to get them, too. The mothers pay me three dollars a week each, and don't have to keep a nursemaid. And I pay ten dollars a week board to Julia, and still have about ten of my own.'

'And she gives music lessons?'

'Yes, she gives music lessons, just as she used to. She loves it, you know. You must have noticed how happy and well she is now — haven't you? And so am I. And so is Albert. You can't feel very badly about a thing that makes us all happy, can you?'

Just then Julia came in, radiant from a brisk walk, fresh and cheery, a big bunch of violets at her breast.

'Oh, Mother,' she cried, 'I've got tickets and we'll all go to hear Melba — if we can get Celia to come in for the evening.'

She saw her husband, and a guilty flush rose to her brow as she met his reproachful eyes.

'Oh, Frank!' she begged, her arms around

his neck. 'Please don't mind! Please get used to it! Please be proud of us! Just think, we're all so happy, and we earn about a hundred dollars a week — all of us together. You see I have Mother's ten to add to the house money, and twenty or more of my own!'

They had a long talk together that evening, just the two of them. She told him, at last, what a danger had hung over them — how near it came.

'And Mother showed me the way out, Frank. The way to have my mind again — and not lose you! She is a different woman herself now that she has her heart and hands full of babies. Albert does enjoy it so! And *you've* enjoyed it — till you found it out!

'And dear — my own love — I don't mind it now at all! I love my home, I love my work, I love my mother, I love you. And as to children — I wish I had six!'

He looked at her flushed, eager, lovely face, and drew her close to him.

'If it makes all of you as happy as that,' he said, 'I guess I can stand it.'

And in after years he was heard to remark, 'This being married and bringing up children is as easy as can be — when you learn how!'

Girls and Land

If Dacia Boone's father had lived he would have been a rich man, a very rich man, and a power in politics also — for good or ill. He was of the same stamp as Mark Hanna, a born organizer, an accumulator and efficient handler of money. His widow was deeply convinced of this, and expressed her opinion with explicit firmness, more rather than less as the years advanced.

She expressed it to Dacia and her older sisters from infancy up; to all her friends, relatives and associates; and, unfortunately, to Mr Ordway, her second husband. He was, as she would plaintively explain, a far nicer man to live with than Her First; but he had no gift for making money — which was entirely true. He managed to feed and clothe her three Boone daughters, and the later brood of little Ordways, also to give them a chance at an education, but that appeared to be his limit.

They moved from place to place, in search of better fortune, urged always by the uneasy mother. She seemed to feel that if he could only find his proper place and work he would do well, but as a matter of fact he did fairly well in each attempt, and never any better.

When Dacia was twenty the family had a homestead in the state of Washington, a big fertile place, lacking only a good road to the nearest station to be a profitable fruit ranch. Of this ranch they had hopes, high, but distant. For the rest they lived in a small house on one of Seattle's many hills, and Mr Ordway worked at what jobs he could get, — as a foreman, manager, small contractor. He had experience enough for a dozen; he could handle men, he was honest and efficient; but blind to the various side issues wherein other men made money.

The two older girls were married, and using what powers they had to spur their husbands on toward high financial achievements; but as for Dacia — she worked in a store. Her mother had opposed it, naturally; but the girl was quietly persistent, and usually got her way.

'Oh, what's the use, mother!' she said. 'I shan't marry — I'm too homely, you know that.'

'It's not your looks, my dear child,' Mrs Ordway would mournfully reply. 'There's plenty of homelier girls than you are — much homelier — that marry. But it is the way you act — you somehow don't try to be — attractive.'

Dacia smiled her wide, good-natured smile. 'No, I don't, and what's more, I won't. So what between lack of beauty and lack of attractiveness — '

'And lack of money!' her mother broke in. 'If your father had only lived!'

'I don't believe I could have loved him any better than I do the father I've got,' said the girl loyally. As a matter of fact, for all her frequent references to the departed, the only salient point his widow ever mentioned was that capacity of his for making money.

Dacia went to work, trying several trades, and was in a good position as saleswoman — she flatly refused to say 'saleslady' — by the time she was twenty.

She was homely. A strong, square, dark face, determined and good-natured, but in no way beautiful; rather a heavy figure, but sturdy and active; a quiet girl with a close mouth.

'You certainly are the image of your father!' her mother would say; adding with vain pathos: 'If only you had been a man!'

Dacia had no quarrel with being a woman. She had had her woman's experience, too; a deep passionate, wild love for the man who had quite overlooked her and married one of her sisters. They had gone back to Massachusetts to live — for which the lonely girl was

133

deeply thankful. Also she was thankful that no one knew what she had felt, how she had suffered. It was her first great trial in keeping still, and had developed that natural instinct into a settled habit. But though she said little, she thought much; and made plans with a breadth, a length, a daring, that would have made her father proud indeed — had she been a boy.

She saved her money too, steadily laying up a little nest egg for clear purposes of her own. To Mr Ordway she gave a partial confidence.

'Daddy,' said she, 'what do you really think would be the best way to develop our ranch — if we had the money?'

He had ample views on the subject. There were apples, of course; berries — all kinds of fruit. There was market garden ground, flat and rich where the valley spread out a little; the fruit trees grew best on the slopes. There was timber in plenty — if only they had that road to the station! There was power too — a nice little waterfall — all on their land.

'It'll be worth a lot by and by,' he asserted. 'And if only I could raise the capital — but what's the use of talkin'!'

'Lots of use, Daddy dear, if you talk to the right person — such as me! Now tell me something else — who *ought* to build that road?'

'Why, there is a kind of a road — it's laid out all right, as you know — it just needs to be made into a good one. I suppose the town ought to do it, or the county — I don't rightly know.'

'If they furnished the labor, could you manage it, Daddy? Could you build a real good road down to Barville? And how much do you think it would cost?'

'Oh, as to labor — it would take — ' he scribbled a little, with a flat carpenter's pencil, and showed her the estimate. ' 'Twould take that many men, at least,' his blunt forefinger pointing, 'and that long. To pay them — that much; to feed them — that much more — to say nothing of shelter. Are you proposing to go into the road-making business next week, my dear?'

She grinned and shook her head. 'Not next week, Daddy. But I like to know. And you are so practical! If you had the men — and the County let you — you could build that road and be a public benefactor — couldn't you?'

'I could indeed. There's good road metal there too; a stone crusher could be run by that waterfall — or we'd burn the wood for it. Just advance me a hundred thousand dollars or so out of your wages, and I'll do it! But *what's* the use of talkin'!' he repeated.

'Lots of use,' she answered again, 'if I talk

to the right person — such as you!'

Then she said no more on that subject, though he joked her about it when they were alone, and devoted herself to another branch of tactics. She frequented the YWCA, the Social Settlement, one or two churches, and after some months of quiet inquiry found the woman she wanted, a woman with a high enthusiasm for Working Girls' Clubs.

Dacia was interested, became very friendly, said she could get together quite a number, she thought. She brought to this woman the kind of help she needed, earnest capable girls who saw the value of the work, and inside of two years there were established a whole chain of 'R & P Clubs,' self-supporting, and very popular.

R & P? Rest and Pleasure, of course.

With a first group of one hundred girls, paying 25 cents a week, they were sure of $100.00 a month for their rent and furnishing. The same number, paying 20 cents a day for lunch, found to their surprise that half of it fed them, and the remaining half, $60.00 a week, paid for the extra fuel and service, with $10.00 left for profit. When two hundred came to the same place for lunch they laid up $50.00 a week for their sinking fund.

Their big rooms were open in the evening for reading and dancing, for club and class work; and their various young gentleman friends who came to see them there and paid a modest five cents for light refreshment, found it the cheapest good time in the city — and the pleasantest.

The idea spread; Tacoma took it up, and Portland, Bellingham, Everett and Spokane; the larger cities had more than one group.

Meanwhile Dacia went to her father with another modest proposition.

'Daddy,' she urged. 'I've found a nice Swede who is a good carpenter and cabinet maker. He and his wife want a place in the country. Would you be willing to have him cut some of your timber and put up a camp for us — for our clubs, that is — for a Vacation Place?'

'Who's going to pay him?' he asked.

'Oh, I'll pay him, all right; I've got a Fund. But I want you really to sell him a little piece of the property — will you? Just a couple of acres or so, where the garden land is good, and let him pay for it in labor. You can make him agree to sell back to you if he wants to leave.'

This being done, and Dacia allowed to dictate the 'labor,' she set the man to work in good earnest, with some assistants, and soon had camping accommodations for a hundred.

Dacia's Fund, which she had been saving

out of her salary for three years, amounted to $500.00, and served to buy the necessary bedding and other supplies. For further gain, she counted as future asset, a Vacation Fund the Clubs had been saving. There were three now in Seattle, comprising well over four hundred working women, and these had been urged to set aside 25 cents a week for a fortnight's vacation. For this $12.50 of a year's easy saving they were to have transportation and board for two weeks in the hills.

Mrs Olsen, sturdy and industrious, had not been loitering while her husband sawed wood. She had fed him and his assistants; had established a hennery, and a vegetable garden. A few young sheep were kept within safe bounds by a movable wire fence, a device which seemed to Dacia too obvious to avoid, where there were two men to unroll and fasten it to the trees with a quick tap of the hammer, and to reel it up and move it when desired. There were two good cows, also a litter of cheerful young pigs, who basked and grew fat on the little farm.

When it was time for the first detachment of Vacationers, Dacia's fund was all spent, but that hundred times $12.50 was in the savings deposit account of the R & P Clubs, and the girls paid their board with pride and satisfaction. Of the Seattle group of four hundred members, over three hundred had subscribed to this vacation fund; and they came, in self-elected groups, two weeks at a time, all summer long. $3,750.00 they paid in, and when the summer was over Dacia sat down with her father to estimate results of the thirteen weeks.

It had cost $2.40 each to get them there and back with their baggage. To feed them, using the animals on the place and the garden, was not above $2.00 a week. This left $2,430.00. To Mrs Olsen and the sturdy flaxen-braided damsel she had to help her, Dacia paid cash, — $10.00 a week, including the girl's board, but this was only $130.00. Then Dacia paid herself back the $500.00 she had invested, allowed $300.00 for refitting, and had a clear $1,500.00 for her further plans.

Dacia smiled and put it in the bank. She was twenty-two now. That winter she rented a pleasant hall; supplied it with refreshments from the lunch room; had dancing classes established under decent and reasonable management; sublet it for part of the time, and added steadily to her little fund.

Another summer's vacation income, with greater patronage and small additional expense, left her, at twenty-three, with quite a little sum. She had all together her first saving of

$500.00, additional for a year $200.00 (she earned $15.00 a week, boarded for $7.00, dress and incidentals, $3.00 and saved $4.00), the first year's $1,500.00, the winter's additional earning from her rented hall, amounting to $800.00, and the second year's increased income of $1,800.00 — in all $4,800.00.

'Daddy,' said she, 'let's you and me go into the road business. Can't we rent a stone-crusher? How many horses would it need? Don't you think the County will help?'

Mr Ordway went up to the ranch with her and looked over the plant. There were the rough but usable sleeping and eating accommodations, and a small saw and planing mill. There were the Olsens, extremely pleased with themselves. The good wife had earned not only her wages but about half of the board money, paid in for milk, meat, eggs and vegetables. This had gone promptly back to Dacia in payment for their stock, and also enabled them to lay in groceries for the winter. Fuel was plenty and Mr Olsen's two years' work had already covered most of their purchase money.

'But how about labor, Miss Promoter?' asked Mr Ordway. 'Do you realize what it means to feed and pay the force of men we'd need?'

'And how about The Unemployed?' she

answered promptly. 'Some of them are good workmen — and you know how to pick and manage them. If they are sure of shelter and food and steady work, even at moderate pay — don't you think you could get 'em to come?'

Mr Ordway consulted with local officials and other owners of homesteads and timber land in the neighborhood. Everyone wanted the road. Here was some capital offered, waterpower, a competent manager and accommodations for the men. And here was 'The Problem of The Unemployed' looming ahead for the winter. This would remove a little of that difficulty.

So the County was induced to help.

'It's only a drop in the bucket,' said Dacia, 'but if County Canomish can do it, why can't the others? There's Power enough — there's Material enough — there's Brains enough — and there's Labor enough. And a little capital goes a good way, seems to me.'

By spring they had a good hard road, opening up much valuable land and adding much to the prosperity of the whole region; and Dacia had just enough money left, from another winter's earnings and saving, to fumigate and refit her camp.

But that year everything was easier on account of the road, and the greater popularity of the place kept it fuller, and longer open. Five hundred girls and women, in different parties, came up; and Dacia invested one dollar from each $12.50 in improving and beautifying the place, still clearing over $2,500.

She was twenty-four now, and very happy. So was Mr Ordway. He was able to dispose of some of his lumber and start planting the fruit ranch which his heart desired. Mrs Ordway viewed it all with grudging admiration.

'Yes — it's very nice,' she admitted to her daughter. 'Very nice, indeed, but I can't help thinking what your father would have done with a chance like this. But then, he was a man of Financial Genius! If only you had been a boy, Dacia! And if he had only lived to help you!'

'But my second father is helping me,' said Dacia. 'And I'm perfectly willing to be a girl — rather glad I am one, in fact.'

Then she consulted further with Mr Ordway. 'Daddy — can you make furniture out of the kind of wood you've got there?'

'Why, yes — I *could*, I suppose. I never thought of it — plain kitchen sort of furniture. There's not much hard wood.'

'But there's some. And you can set out more, can't you?'

'Set out — ! Plant hardwood trees! Child, you're crazy. Hardwood timber doesn't grow up like lettuce.'

'How long does it take to be — cuttable?'

'Oh — thirty years at least, I should say.'

'Well — let's plant some. It will be valuable when I'm fifty-five or so — and your own children will be younger — they may be glad of it. But meantime I want to propose that you start a little Grand Rapids right by our waterfall there. Can't the mill be turned into a furniture factory? Nice cheap plain furniture — painted or stained — and sold to the folks out here that can't pay the freight on Eastern stuff.'

'Hm!' Mr Ordway considered. He got out his pencil. He made some estimates. 'There's that young Pedersen,' he said, 'the Olsen's cousin — he's a good designer — you've seen what he's made for them?'

Dacia had seen it, and had thought about it quite carefully, but she made no admissions.

'Do you think he'd be useful?'

'I'm pretty sure he would,' said Mr Ordway. 'Dacia, child, you surely have a business head — why there's no real furniture factory on this coast. We might — we might do pretty well, I think.'

Olaf Pedersen thought so too.

'Your wood is much like the wood of our

143

country,' he said. 'And we make furniture. I have no capital, but I will design and work, gladly.'

They began cautiously, with a small workshop, a moderate investment in machinery, and Dacia's big connection of people of small incomes, as advertising ground. She herself had so much faith in the enterprise that she gave up her position and became 'the office force' for the undertaking.

Next year they established the firm of Ordway, Boone & Pedersen. The modesty of their methods was such that they encountered practically no opposition until it was too late to crush them.

'A pleased customer is the best advertisement.' And there were several hundred pleased customers spreading the good news. Furniture that was solid and strong; that was simple, novel and pretty; that was amazingly cheap; that was made right there in their own state — it really pleased the people, and they supported the business.

Even the railroads, finding that their freight payment was as good as others, and that their trade was steadily growing, ceased to be antagonistic.

Mr Ordway settled down to steady work that had a future.

'Dacia,' said he. 'I'm mighty glad that, well,

that I inherited you. You see, I can work and I'm honest, but you've got the brains. You can push.'

'It's Olaf, too, Daddy — it's mostly Olaf — he puts the novelty and beauty into it.'

'Yes, it's Olaf too. You are both good partners. I shall leave the business to you when I go.'

And he did, — to two who were partners of a closer sort long before then; and Boone & Pedersen developed a furniture industry which was of immense service to the whole coast.

If I Were a Man

That was what pretty little Mollie Mathewson always said when Gerald would not do what she wanted him to — which was seldom.

That was what she said this bright morning, with a stamp of her little high-heeled slipper, just because he had made a fuss about that bill, the long one with the 'account rendered,' which she had forgotten to give him the first time and been afraid to the second — and now he had taken it from the postman himself.

Mollie was 'true to type.' She was a beautiful instance of what is reverentially called 'a true woman.' Little, of course — no true woman may be big. Pretty, of course — no true woman could possibly be plain. Whimsical, capricious, charming, changeable, devoted to pretty clothes and always 'wearing them well,' as the esoteric phrase has it. (This does not refer to the clothes — they do not wear well in the least; but to some special grace of putting them on and carrying them about, granted to but few, it appears.)

She was also a loving wife and a devoted mother; possessed of 'the social gift' and the love of 'society' that goes with it, and, with all these was fond and proud of her home and managed it as capably as — well, as most women do.

If ever there was a true woman it was Mollie Mathewson, yet she was wishing heart and soul she was a man.

And all of a sudden she was!

She was Gerald, walking down the path so erect and square-shouldered, in a hurry for his morning train, as usual, and, it must be confessed, in something of a temper.

Her own words were ringing in her ears — not only the 'last word,' but several that had gone before, and she was holding her lips tight shut, not to say something she would be sorry for. But instead of acquiescence in the position taken by that angry little figure on the veranda, what she felt was a sort of superior pride, a sympathy as with weakness, a feeling that 'I must be gentle with her,' in spite of the temper.

A man! Really a man; with only enough subconscious memory of herself remaining to make her recognize the differences.

At first there was a funny sense of size and weight and extra thickness, the feet and hands seemed strangely large, and her long, straight, free legs swung forward at a gait that made her feel as if on stilts.

This presently passed, and in its place, growing all day, wherever she went, came a new and delightful feeling of being *the right size.*

Everything fitted now. Her back snugly against the seat-back, her feet comfortably on the floor. Her feet? . . . His feet! She studied them carefully. Never before, since her early school days, had she felt such freedom and comfort as to feet — they were firm and solid on the ground when she walked; quick, springy, safe — as when, moved by an unrecognizable impulse, she had run after, caught, and swung aboard the car.

Another impulse fished in a convenient pocket for change — instantly, automatically, bringing forth a nickel for the conductor and a penny for the newsboy.

These pockets came as a revelation. Of course she had known they were there, had counted them, made fun of them, mended them, even envied them; but she never had dreamed of how it *felt* to have pockets.

Behind her newspaper she let her consciousness, that odd mingled consciousness, rove from pocket to pocket, realizing the armored assurance of having all those things at hand, instantly get-at-able, ready to meet emergencies. The cigar case gave her a warm feeling of comfort — it was full; the firmly

151

held fountain-pen, safe unless she stood on her head; the keys, pencils, letters, documents, notebook, checkbook, bill folder — all at once, with a deep rushing sense of power and pride, she felt what she had never felt before in all her life — the possession of money, of her own earned money — hers to give or to withhold; not to beg for, tease for, wheedle for — hers.

That bill — why if it had come to her — to him, that is, he would have paid it as a matter of course, and never mentioned it — to her.

Then, being he, sitting there so easily and firmly with his money in his pockets, she wakened to his life-long consciousness about money. Boyhood — its desires and dreams, ambitions. Young manhood — working tremendously for the wherewithal to make a home — for her. The present years with all their net of cares and hopes and dangers; the present moment, when he needed every cent for special plans of great importance, and this bill, long overdue and demanding payment, meant an amount of inconvenience wholly unnecessary if it had been given him when it first came; also, the man's keen dislike of that 'account rendered.'

'Women have no business sense!' she found herself saying, 'and all that money just for hats — idiotic, useless, ugly things!'

With that she began to see the hats of the women in the car as she had never seen hats before. The men's seemed normal, dignified, becoming, with enough variety for personal taste, and with distinction in style and in age, such as she had never noticed before. But the women's —

With the eyes of a man and the brain of a man; with the memory of a whole lifetime of free action wherein the hat, close-fitting on cropped hair, had been no handicap; she now perceived the hats of women.

Their massed fluffed hair was at once attractive and foolish, and on that hair, at every angle, in all colors, tipped, twisted, tortured into every crooked shape, made of any substance chance might offer, perched these formless objects. Then, on their formlessness the trimmings — these squirts of stiff feathers, these violent outstanding bows of glistening ribbon, these swaying, projecting masses of plumage which tormented the faces of bystanders.

Never in all her life had she imagined that this idolized millinery could look, to those who paid for it, like the decorations of an insane monkey.

And yet, when there came into the car a little woman, as foolish as any, but pretty and sweet-looking, up rose Gerald Mathewson and gave her his seat; and, later, when there came in a handsome red-cheeked girl, whose hat was wilder, more violent in color and eccentric in shape than any other; when she stood near by and her soft curling plumes swept his cheek once and again, he felt a sense of sudden pleasure at the intimate tickling touch — and she, deep down within, felt such a wave of shame as might well drown a thousand hats forever.

When he took his train, his seat in the smoking car, she had a new surprise. All about him were the other men, commuters too, and many of them friends of his.

To her, they would have been distinguished as 'Mary Wade's husband' — 'the man Belle Grant is engaged to' — 'that rich Mr Shopworth' — or 'that pleasant Mr Beale.' And they would all have lifted their hats to her, bowed, made polite conversation if near enough — especially Mr Beale.

Now came the feeling of open-eyed acquaintance, of knowing men — as they were. The mere amount of this knowledge was a surprise to her; the whole background of talk from boyhood up, the gossip of barber-shop and club, the conversation of morning and evening hours on trains, the knowledge of political affiliation, of business standing and prospects, of character — in a light she had never known before.

They came and talked to Gerald, one and another. He seemed quite popular. And as they talked, with this new memory and new understanding, an understanding which seemed to include all these men's minds, there poured in on the submerged consciousness beneath a new, a startling knowledge — what men really think of women.

Good average American men were there; married men for the most part, and happy — as happiness goes in general. In the minds of each and all there seemed to be a two-story department, quite apart from the rest of their ideas, a separate place where they kept their thoughts and feelings about women.

In the upper half were the tenderest emotions, the most exquisite ideals, the sweetest memories, all lovely sentiments as to 'home' and 'mother,' all delicate admiring adjectives, a sort of sanctuary, where a veiled statue, blindly adored, shared place with beloved yet commonplace experiences.

In the lower half — here that buried consciousness woke to keen distress — they kept quite another assortment of ideas. Here, even in this clean-minded husband of hers, was the memory of stories told at men's dinners, of worse ones overheard in street or car, of base traditions, coarse epithets, gross

155

experiences — known, though not shared.

And all these in the department 'woman,' while in the rest of the mind — here was new knowledge indeed.

The world opened before her. Not the world she had been reared in; where Home had covered all the map, almost, and the rest had been 'foreign,' or 'unexplored country;' but the world as it was, man's world, as made, lived in, and seen, by men.

It was dizzying. To see the houses that fled so fast across the car window, in terms of builders' bills, or of some technical insight into materials and methods; to see a passing village with lamentable knowledge of who 'owned it' — and of how its Boss was rapidly aspiring to State power, or of how that kind of paving was a failure; to see shops, not as mere exhibitions of desirable objects, but as business ventures, many mere sinking ships, some promising a profitable voyage — this new world bewildered her.

She — as Gerald — had already forgotten about that bill, over which she — as Mollie — was still crying at home. Gerald was 'talking business' with this man, 'talking politics' with that; and now sympathizing with the carefully withheld troubles of a neighbor.

Mollie had always sympathized with the neighbor's wife before.

She began to struggle violently, with this large dominant masculine consciousness. She remembered with sudden clearness things she had read — lectures she had heard; and resented with increasing intensity this serene masculine preoccupation with the male point of view.

Mr Miles, the little fussy man who lived on the other side of the street, was talking now. He had a large complacent wife; Mollie had never liked her much, but had always thought him rather nice — he was so punctilious in small courtesies.

And here he was talking to Gerald — such talk!

'Had to come in here,' he said. 'Gave my seat to a dame who was bound to have it. There's nothing they won't get when they make up their minds to it — eh?'

'No fear!' said the big man in the next seat, 'they haven't much mind to make up, you know — and if they do, they'll change it.'

'The real danger,' began the Revd Alfred Smythe, the new Episcopal clergyman, a thin, nervous, tall man, with a face several centuries behind the times, 'is that they will overstep the limits of their God-appointed sphere.'

'Their natural limits ought to hold 'em, I think,' said cheerful Dr Jones. 'You can't get around physiology, I tell you.'

'I've never seen any limits, myself, not to what they want, anyhow;' said Mr Miles, 'merely a rich husband and a fine house and no end of bonnets and dresses, and the latest thing in motors, and a few diamonds — and so on. Keeps us pretty busy.'

There was a tired gray man across the aisle. He had a very nice wife, always beautifully dressed, and three unmarried daughters, also beautifully dressed — Mollie knew them. She knew he worked hard too, and looked at him now a little anxiously.

But he smiled cheerfully.

'Do you good, Miles,' he said. 'What else would a man work for? A good woman is about the best thing on earth.'

'And a bad one's the worst, that's sure,' responded Miles.

'She's a pretty weak sister, viewed professionally,' Dr Jones averred with solemnity, and the Revd Alfred Smythe added: 'She brought evil into the world.'

Gerald Mathewson sat up straight. Something was stirring in him which he did not recognize — yet could not resist.

'Seems to me we all talk like Noah,' he suggested drily. 'Or the ancient Hindu scriptures. Women have their limitations, but so do we, God knows. Haven't we known girls in school and college just as smart as we were?'

'They cannot play our games,' coldly replied the clergyman.

Gerald measured his meager proportions with a practiced eye.

'I never was particularly good at football myself,' he modestly admitted, 'but I've known women who could outlast a man in all-round endurance. Besides — life isn't spent in athletics!'

This was sadly true. They all looked down the aisle where a heavy ill-dressed man with a bad complexion sat alone. He had held the top of the columns once, with headlines and photographs. Now he earned less than any of them.

'It's time we woke up,' pursued Gerald, still inwardly urged to unfamiliar speech. 'Women are pretty much *people*, seems to me. I know they dress like fools — but who's to blame for that? We invent all those idiotic hats of theirs, and design their crazy fashions, and, what's more, if a woman is courageous enough to wear common sense clothes — and shoes — which of us wants to dance with her?

'Yes, we blame them for grafting on us, but are we willing to let our wives work? We are not. It hurts our pride, that's all. We are always criticizing them for making mercenary marriages, but what do we call a girl who marries a chump with no money? Just a poor

159

fool, that's all. And they know it.

'As for those physical limitations, Dr Jones, I guess our side of the house has some responsibility there, too — eh?

'And for Mother Eve — I wasn't there and can't deny the story, but I will say this, if she brought evil into the world we men have had the lion's share of keeping it going ever since — how about that?'

They drew into the city, and all day long in his business, Gerald was vaguely conscious of new views, strange feelings, and the submerged Mollie learned and learned.

Mrs Merrill's Duties

Grace Leroy, in college, was quite the most important member of the class. She had what her professors proudly pointed out as the rarest thing among women — a scientific mind. The arts had no charms for her; she had no wish to teach, no leaning toward that branch of investigation and alleviation in social pathology we are so apt to call 'social service.'

Her strength was in genuine research work, and, back of that, greatest gift of all, she showed high promise in 'the scientific imagination,' the creative synthesizing ability which gives new discoveries to the world.

In addition to these natural advantages a merciful misfortune saved her from the widespread silvery quicksand which so often engulfs the girl graduate. Instead of going home to decorate the drawing-room and help her mother receive, she was obliged to go to work at once, owing to paternal business difficulties.

Her special teacher, old Dr Welsch, succeeded in getting a laboratory position for her; and for three years she worked side by side with a great chemist and physicist, Dr Hammerton, his most valued assistant.

She was very happy.

Happy, of course, to be useful to her family at once, instead of an added burden. Happy in her sense of independence and a real place in the world; happy in the feeling of personal power and legitimate pride of achievement. Happiest of all in the brightening dawn of great ideas, big glittering hopes of a discovery that should lighten humanity's burdens. Hardly did she dare to hope for it, yet it did seem almost possible at times. Being of a truly religious nature she prayed earnestly over this; to be good enough to deserve the honor; to keep humble and not overestimate her powers; to be helped to do the Great Work.

Then Life rolled swiftly along and swept her off her feet.

Her father recovered his money and her mother lost her health. For a time there seemed absolute need of her at home.

'I must not neglect plain duty,' said the girl, and resigned her position.

There was a year of managing the household, with the care of younger brothers and sisters; a year of travel with the frail mother, drifting slowly from place to place, from physician to physician, always hoping, and always being disappointed.

Then came the grief of losing her, after they had grown so close, so deeply, tenderly intimate.

'Whatever happens,' said Grace to herself, 'I shall always be glad of these two years. No outside work could justify me in neglecting this primal duty.'

What did happen next was her father's turning to her for comfort. She alone could in any degree take her mother's place to him. He could not bear to think of her as leaving the guidance of the family. His dependence was touching.

Grace accepted the new duty bravely.

There was the year of deep mourning, both in symbolic garments and observances and in the real sorrow; and she found herself learning to know her father better than she ever had, and learning how to somewhat make up to him for the companionship he had lost. There was the need of mothering the younger ones, of managing the big house.

Then came the next sister's debut, and the cares and responsibilities involved. Another sister was growing up, and the young brother called for sympathetic guidance. There seemed no end to it.

She bowed her head and faced her duty.

'Nothing can be right,' she said, 'which

would take me away from these intimate claims.'

Everyone agreed with her in this.

Her father was understanding and tender in his thoughtfulness.

'I know what a sacrifice you are making, daughter, in giving up your chemistry, but what could I do without you! . . . You are so much like your mother . . . '

As time passed she did speak once or twice of a housekeeper, that she might have some free hours during the day-time, but he was so hurt at the idea that she gave it up.

Then something happened that proved with absurd ease the fallacy of the fond conclusion that nothing could be right which would take her away. Hugh Merrill took her away, and that was accepted by everyone as perfectly right.

She had known him a long time, but had hardly dared let herself think of marrying him — she was so indispensable at home. But when his patience and his ardor combined finally swept her off her feet; when her father said: 'Why, of course, my child! Hugh is a splendid fellow! We shall miss you — but do you think I would stand in the way of your happiness!' — she consented. She raised objections about the housekeeping, but her father promptly met them by installing a widowed sister, Aunt Adelaide, who had always been a favorite with them all.

She managed the home quite as well, and the children really better, than had Grace; and she and her brother played cribbage and backgammon in the evenings with pleasant reversion to their youthful comradeship — he seemed to grow younger for having her there.

Grace was so happy, so relieved by the sudden change from being the mainstay of four other people and a big house to being considered and cared for in every way by a strong resourceful affectionate man, that she did not philosophize at all at the easy dispensibility of the indispensable.

With Hugh she rested; regained her youth, bloomed like a flower. There was a long delightful journey; a pleasant homecoming; the setting up of her very own establishment; the cordial welcome from her many friends.

In all this she never lost sight of her inner hope of the Great Work.

Hugh had profound faith in her. They talked of it on their long honeymoon, in full accord. She should have her laboratory, she should work away at her leisure, she would do wonderful things — he was sure of it.

But that first year was so full of other things, so crowded with invitations, so crowded with careful consideration of clothes and menus and servants, the duties of a hostess, or a guest — that the big room upstairs was not yet a laboratory.

An unexpected illness with its convalescence took another long period; she needed rest, a change. Another year went by.

Grace was about thirty now.

Then the babies came — little Hugh and Arnold — splendid boys. A happier, prouder mother one would not wish to see. She thanked God with all her heart; she felt the deep and tender oneness with her husband that comes of parentage, with reverent joy.

To the task of education she now devoted her warmly loving heart, her clear strong mind. It was noble work. She neglected nothing. This duty was imperative. No low-grade nursemaid should, through ignorance, do some irremediable injury to opening baby minds.

With the help of a fully competent assistant, expensive, but worth all she cost, Mrs Merrill brought up those boys herself, and the result should have satisfied even the most exacting educator. Hearty, well-grown, unaffected, with clear minds and beautiful manners, they grew up to sturdy boyhood, taking high places when they went to school; loved by their teachers, comrades and friends, and everyone said: 'What a lovely mother she is!'

She did not admit to anyone that even in this period of lovely mothering, even with the home happiness, the wife happiness, the pleasant social position, there was still an aching want inside. She wanted her laboratory, her research, her work. All her years of education, from the first chemistry lessons at fourteen to the giving up of her position at twenty-four, had made her a chemist, and nature had made her a discoverer.

She had not read much during these years; it hurt her — made her feel an exile. She had shut the door on all that side of her life, and patiently, gladly fulfilled the duties of the other side, neglecting nothing.

Not till ten more years had passed did she draw a long breath and say: 'Now I will have my laboratory!'

She had it. There was the big room, all this time a nursery; now at last fitted up with all the mysterious implements and supplies of her chosen profession.

The boys were at school — her husband at his business — now she could concentrate on the Great Work.

And then Mrs Merrill began to realize 'the defects of her qualities.'

There is such a thing as being too good.

We all know that little one-handed tool combination which carries in its inside screw-driver, gouge and chisel, awl and file — a marvellously handy thing to have in the house. Yes — but did you ever see a carpenter use one? The real workman, for real work, must have real tools, of which the value is, not that they will all fit one hollow and feeble handle, but that each will do what it is meant for, well.

We have seen in Grace Leroy Merrill the strength of mind and character, Christian submission, filial duty, wifely love, motherly efficiency. She had other qualities also, all pleasant ones. She was a pre-eminently attractive woman, more than pretty — charming. She was sweet and cordial in manner, quick and witty, a pleasure to talk with for either man or woman. Add to these the possession of special talent for dress, and a gentle friendliness that could not bear to hurt anyone, and we begin to feel 'this is too much. No person has a right to be so faultless, so universally efficient and attractive.'

Social psychology is a bit complicated. We need qualities, not only valuable for personal, but for social relation. In the growing complexity of a highly specialized organization the law of organic specialization calls for a varying degree of sacrifice in personal fulfillment. It is quite possible, indeed it is usual, to find individuals whose numerous good qualities really stand in the way of their best service to society. The best tools are not those of the greatest 'all round' variety of usefulness.

When the boys were grown up enough to be off her mind for many hours a day; when the house fairly ran itself in the hands of well-trained servants; when, at last, the laboratory was installed and the way seemed open; Mrs Merrill found herself fairly bogged in her own popularity. She had so many friends; they were so unfailingly anxious to have her at their dinners, their dances, their continuous card parties; they came to her so confidingly, so frequently — and she could never bear to hurt their feelings.

There were, to be sure, mornings. One is not required to play bridge in the morning, or dance, or go to the theatre. But even the daily ordering for a household takes some time, and besides the meals there are the supplies in clothing, linen, china; and the spring and fall extras of putting things away with mothballs, having rugs cleaned and so on — and so on.

Then — clothes; her own clothes. The time to think about them; the time to discuss them; the time to buy them; the time to stand up and be fitted — to plan and struggle with the dressmaker — a great deal of time — and no sooner is the feat accomplished than

— presto! — it must be done all over.

Day after day she mounted the stairs to her long looked-for work-room, with an hour — or two — or three — before her. Day after day she was called down again; friends at the telephone, friends at the door; friends who were full of cheerful apology and hopes that they did not disturb her; and tradesmen who were void of either.

'If only I could get something *done!*' she said, as she sat staring at her retorts. 'If once I could really accomplish a piece of good work, that should command public acknowledgement — then they would understand. Then I could withdraw from all this — '

For she found that her hours were too few, and too broken, to allow of that concentration of mind without which no great work is possible.

But she was a strong woman, a patient woman, and possessed of a rich fund of perseverance. With long waiting, with careful use of summer months when her too devoted friends were out of town, she managed in another five years, to really accomplish something. From her little laboratory, working alone and under all distractions, she finally sent out a new formula; not for an explosive of deadly power, but for a safe and simple sedative, something which induced natural sleep, with no ill results.

It was no patented secret. She gave it to the world with the true scientific spirit, and her joy was like that of motherhood. She had at last achieved! She had done something — something of real service to thousands upon thousands. And back of this first little hill, so long in winning, mountain upon mountain, range on range, rose hopefully tempting before her.

She was stronger now. She had gotten back into the lines of study, of persistent work. Her whole mind stirred and freshened with new ideas, high purposes. She planned for further research, along different lines. Two Great Ones tempted her; a cheap combustible fluid; and that biggest prize of all — the mastering of atomic energy.

And now, now that she had really made this useful discovery, which was widely recognized among those who knew of such matters, she could begin to protect herself from these many outside calls!

★　★　★

What did happen?

She found herself quite lionized for a season — name in the papers, pictures, interviews, and a whole series of dinners and receptions where she was wearied beyond measure by the well-meant comments on her work.

Free? Respected? Let alone?

Her hundreds of friends, who had known her so long and so well, as a charming girl, a devoted daughter, an irreproachable wife, a most unusually successful mother, were only the more cordial now.

'Have you heard about Grace Merrill? Isn't it wonderful! She always had ability — I've always said so.'

'Such a service to the world! A new anesthetic!'

'Oh, it's not an anesthetic — not really.'

'Like the Twilight Sleep, I imagine.'

'It's splendid of her anyway. I've asked her to dinner Thursday, to meet Professor Andrews — he's an authority on dietetics, you know, and Dr North and his wife — they are such interesting people!'

★ ★ ★

Forty-six! Still beautiful, still charming, still exquisitely gowned. Still a happy wife and mother, with Something Done — at last.

And yet —

Her next younger sister, who had lost her husband and was greatly out of health, now wanted to come and live with her; their father had followed his wife some years back and the old home was broken up.

That meant being tied up at home again. And as to the social engagements, she was more hopelessly popular than ever.

Then one day there came to see her Dr Hammerton. His brush of hair was quite white, but thick and erect as ever. His keen black eyes sparkled portentously under thick white eyebrows.

'What's this you've been doing, Child? Show me your shop.'

She showed him, feeling very girlish again in the presence of her early master. He looked the place over in silence, told her he had read about her new product, sat on the edge of a table and made her take a chair.

'Now tell me about it!' he said.

She told him — all about it. He listened, nodding agreeably as she recounted the steps.

'Mother? Yes. Father? Yes — for awhile at least. Husband? Yes. Boys? Of course — and you've done well. But what's the matter now?'

She told him that too — urging her hope of forcing some acknowledgment by her proven ability.

He threw back his big head and laughed.

'You've got the best head of any woman I ever saw,' he said; 'you've done what not one woman in a thousand does — kept a living Self able to survive family relations. You've

175

proven, now, that you are still in the ring. You ought to do — twenty — maybe thirty years of worthwhile work. Forty-six? I was forty-eight when you left me, have done my best work since then, am seventy now, and am still going strong. You've spent twenty-two years in worthwhile woman-work that's *done* — now you have at least as much again to do human work. I daresay you'll do better because of all this daughtering and mothering — women are queer things. Anyhow you've plenty of time. But you must get to work.

'Now, see here — if you let all these childish flub-dubs prevent you from doing what God made you for — you're a Criminal Fool!'

Grace gave a little gasp.

'I mean it. You know it. It's all nonsense, empty nonsense. As for your sister — let her go to a sanitarium — she can afford it, or live with her other sister — or brother. You've earned your freedom.

'As to clothes and parties — Quit!'

She looked at him.

'Yes, I know. You're still pretty and attractive, but *what of it?* Suppose Spencer or Darwin had wasted their time as parlor ornaments — supposing they could have — would they have had a right to?'

She caught at the names. 'You think I could do something — Great?' she asked. 'You think I am — big enough — to try?'

He stood up. She rose and faced him.

'I think you are great, to have done what you have — a task no man could face. I think you will be greater — perhaps one of the big World Helpers.' Then his eyes shot fire — and he thundered: 'How Dare you hinder the World's Work by wasting your time with these idle women? It is Treason — High Treason — to Humanity.'

'What can I do?' she asked at last.

'That's a foolish question, child. Use your brain — you've got plenty. Learn to assert yourself and stand up to it, that's all. Tell your sister you can't. Disconnect the telephone. Hire some stony-faced menial to answer the door and say: 'Mrs Merrill is engaged. She left orders not to be disturbed.'

'Decide on how many evenings you can afford to lose sleep, and decline to go out on all others. It's simple enough.

'But you've got to *do it*. You've got to plan it and stand by it. It takes Courage — and it takes Strength.'

'But if it is my duty — ' said Grace Merrill.

The old man smiled and left her. 'Once that woman sees a Duty!' he said to himself.

Joan's Defender

Joan's mother was a poor defense. Her maternal instinct did not present that unbroken front of sterling courage, that measureless reserve of patience, that unfailing wisdom which we are taught to expect of it. Rather a broken reed was Mrs Marsden, broken in spirit even before her health gave way, and her feeble nerves were unable to stand the strain of adjudicating the constant difficulties between Joan and Gerald.

'Mother! Mo-o-ther!' would rise a protesting wail from the little girl. 'Gerald's pulling my hair!'

'Cry baby!' her brother would promptly retort. 'Tell tale! Run to mother — do!'

Joan did — there was no one else to run to — but she got small comfort.

'One of you is as much to blame as the other,' the invalid would proclaim. And if this did not seem to help much: 'If he teases you, go into another room!'

Whether Mrs Marsden supposed that her daughter was a movable body and her son a fixed star as it were, did not appear, but there was small comfort to be got from her.

'If you can't play nicely together you must be separated. If I hear anything more from you I'll send you to your room — now be quiet!'

So Joan sulked, helplessly, submitted to much that was painful and more that was contumelious, and made little remonstrance. There was, of course, a last court of appeal, or rather a last threat — that of telling father.

'I'll tell father! I'll tell father! Then you'll be sorry!' her tormentor would chant, jumping nimbly about just out of reach, if she had succeeded in any overt act of vengeance.

'I shall have to tell your father!' was the last resource of the mother on the sofa.

If father was told, no matter by whom, the result was always the same — he whipped them both. Not so violently, to be sure, and Joan secretly believed less violently in Gerald's case than in hers, but it was an ignominious and unsatisfying punishment which both avoided.

'Can't you manage to keep two children in order?' he would demand of his wife. 'My mother managed eleven — and did the work of the house too.'

'I wish I could, Bert, dear,' she would meekly reply. 'I do try — but they are so wearying. Gerald is too rough, I'm afraid. Joan is always complaining.'

'I should think she was!' Mr Marsden agreed irritably. 'Trust a woman for that!'

And Joan, though but nine years old, felt that life was not worth living, being utterly unjust. She was a rather large-boned, meager child, with a whiney voice, and a habit of crying, 'Now stop!' whenever Gerald touched her. Her hair was long, fine and curly, a great trouble to her as well as to her mother. Both were generally on edge for the day, before those curls were all in order, and their principal use appeared to be as handles for Gerald, who was always pulling them. He was a year and a half older than Joan, but not much bigger, and of a somewhat puny build.

Their father, a burly, loud-voiced man, heavy of foot and of hand, looked at them both with ill-concealed disapproval, and did not hesitate to attribute the general deficiencies of his family wholly to their feeble mother and her 'side of the house.'

'I'm sure I was strong as a girl, Bert — you remember how I used to play tennis, and I could dance all night.'

'Oh I remember,' he would answer. 'Blaming your poor health on me, I suppose — that seems to be the way nowadays. I don't notice that other women give out just because they're married and have two children — *two!*' he repeated scornfully, as if Mrs

Marsden's product were wholly negligible. 'And one of them a girl!'

'Girls are no good!' Gerald quickly seconded. 'Girls can't fight or climb or do anything. And they're always hollering. Huh! I wouldn't be a girl — !' Words failed him.

Such was their case, as it says so often in the *Arabian Nights*, and then something pleasant happened. Uncle Arthur came for a little visit, and Joan liked him. He was mother's brother, not father's. He was big, like father, but gentle and pleasant, and he had such a nice voice, jolly but not loud.

Uncle Arthur was a western man, with a ranch, and a large family of his own. He had begun life as a physician, but weak lungs drove him into the open. No one would ever think of him now as ever having been an invalid.

He stayed for a week or so, having some business to settle which dragged on for more days than had been counted on, and gave careful attention to the whole family.

Joan was not old enough, nor Mrs Marsden acute enough, to note the gradual disappearance of topic after topic from the conversation between Uncle Arthur and his host. But Mr Marsden's idea of argument was volume of sound, speed in repetition, and a visible scorn for those who disagreed with him, and as Arthur Warren did not excel in these methods he sought for subjects of agreement. Not finding any, he contented himself with telling stories, or listening — for which there was large opportunity.

He bought sweetmeats for the children, and observed that Gerald got three-quarters, if not more; brought them presents, and found that, if Gerald did not enjoy playing with Joan's toys, he did enjoy breaking them.

He sounded Gerald, as man to man, in regard to these habits, but that loyal son, who believed his father to be a type of all that was worthy, and who secretly had assumed the attitude of scorn adopted by that parent toward his visitor, although civil enough, was little moved by anything his uncle might say.

Dr Warren was not at all severe with him. He believed in giving a child the benefit of every doubt, and especially the benefit of time.

'How can the youngster help being a pig?' he asked himself, sitting quite silent and watching Gerald play ball with a book just given to Joan, who cried 'Now sto-op!' and tried to get it away from him.

'Madge Warren Marsden!' he began very seriously, when the children were quarreling mildly in the garden, and the house was quiet: 'Do you think you're doing right by Joan — let alone Gerald? Is there no way that boy can be made to treat his sister decently?'

'Of course you take her part — I knew you would,' she answered fretfully. 'You always were partial to girls — having so many of your own, I suppose. But you've no idea how irritating Joan is, and Gerald is extremely sensitive — she gets on his nerves. As for *my* nerves! I have none left! Of course those children ought to be separated. By and by when we can afford it, we mean to send Gerald to a good school; he's a very bright boy — you must have noticed that?'

'Oh yes, he's bright enough,' her brother agreed. 'And so is Joan, for that matter. But look here, Madge — this thing is pretty hard on you, isn't it — having these two irreconcilables to manage all the time?'

The ready tears rose and ran over. 'Oh Arthur, it's awful! I do my best — but I never was good with children — and with my nerves — *you* know, being a doctor.'

He did know, rather more than she gave him credit for. She had responded to his interest with interminable details as to her symptoms and sensations, and while he sat patiently listening he had made a diagnosis which was fairly accurate. Nothing in particular was the matter with his sister except the fretful temper she was born with, idle habits, and the effects of an overbearing husband.

The temper he could not alter, the habits he could not change, nor the husband either, so he gave her up — she was out of his reach.

But Joan was a different proposition. Joan had his mother's eyes, his mother's smile — when she did smile; and though thin and nervous, she had no serious physical disability as yet.

'Joan worries you even more than Gerald, doesn't she?' he ventured. 'It's often so with mothers.'

'How well you understand, Arthur. Yes, indeed, I feel as if I knew just what to do with my boy, but Joan is a puzzle. She is so — unresponsive.'

'Seems to me you would be much stronger if you were less worried over the children.'

'Of course — but what can I do? It is my duty and I hope I can hold out.'

'For the children's sake you ought to be stronger, Madge. See here, suppose you lend me Joan for a long visit. It would be no trouble at all to us — we have eight, you know, and all outdoors for them to romp in. I think it would do the child good.'

The mother looked uncertain. 'It's a long way to let her go — ' she said.

'And it would do Gerald good, I verily believe,' her brother continued. 'I've often heard you say that she irritates him.'

He could not bring himself to advance this opinion, but he could quote it.

'She does indeed, Arthur. I think Gerald would give almost no trouble if he was alone.'

'And you are of some importance,' he continued cheerfully. 'How about that? Let me borrow Joan for a year — you'll be another woman when you get rested.'

There was a good deal of discussion, and sturdy opposition from Mr Marsden, who considered the feelings of a father quite outraged by the proposal; but as Dr Warren did not push it, and as his wife suggested that in one way it would be an advantage — they could save toward Gerald's schooling — adding that her brother meant to pay all expenses, including tickets — he finally consented.

Joan was unaccountably reluctant. She clung to her mother, who said, 'There! There!' and kissed her with much emotion. 'It's only a visit, dearie — you'll be back to mother bye and bye!'

She kissed her father, who told her to be a good girl and mind her uncle and aunt. She would have kissed Gerald, but he said: 'Oh shucks!' and drew away from her.

It was a silently snivelling little girl who sat by the window, with Uncle Arthur reading the paper beside her, a little girl who felt as if nobody loved her in the whole wide world. He put a big arm around her and drew her to him. She snuggled up with a long sigh of relief. He took her in his lap, held her close, and told her interesting things about the flying landscape. She nestled close to him, and then, starting up suddenly to look at something, her hair caught on his buttons and pulled sharply.

She cried, as was her habit, while he disentangled it.

'How'd you like to have it cut off?' he asked.

'*I'd* like it — but mother won't let me. She says it's my only beauty. And father won't let me either — says I want to be a tom-boy.'

'Well, I'm in loco parentis now,' said Uncle Arthur, 'and I'll let you. Furthermore, I'll do it forthwith, before it gets tangled up to-night.'

He produced a pair of sharp little scissors, and a pocket-comb, and in a few minutes the small head looked like one of Sir Joshua Reynold's cherubs.

'You see I know how,' he explained, as he snipped cautiously, 'because I cut my own youngsters' on the ranch. I think you look prettier short than long,' he told her, and she found the little mirror between the windows quite a comfort.

Before the end of that long journey the

child was more quietly happy with her uncle than she had ever been with either father or mother, and as for Gerald — the doctor's wise smile deepened.

'Irritated *him*, did she?' he murmured to himself. 'The little skate! Why, I can just see her *heal* now she's escaped.'

A big, high-lying California ranch, broad, restful sweeps of mesa and plain, purple hills rising behind. Flowers beyond dreams of heaven, fruit of every kind in gorgeous abundance. A cheerful Chinese cook and houseboy, who did their work well and seemed to enjoy it. The uncle she already loved, and an aunt who took her to her motherly heart at once.

Then the cousins — here was terror. And four of them boys — four! But which four? There they all were in a row, giggling happily, standing up to be counted, and to be introduced to their new cousin. All had short hair. All had bare feet. All had denim knicker-bockers. And all had been racing and tumbling and turning somersaults on the cushiony Bermuda grass as Joan and her uncle drove up.

The biggest one was a girl, tall Hilda, and the baby was a girl, a darling dimpled thing, and two of the middle ones. But the four boys were quite as friendly as Hilda, and seeing that their visitor was strangely shy, Jack promptly proposed to show her his Belgian hares, and Harvey to exhibit his Angora goats, and the whole of them trooped off hilariously.

'What a forlorn child!' said Aunt Belle. 'I'm glad you brought her, dear. Ours will do her good.'

'I knew you'd mother her, Blessing,' he said with a grateful kiss. 'And if ever a poor kid needed mothering, it's that one. You see, my sister has married a noisy pig of a man — and doesn't seem to mind it much. But she's become an invalid — one of these sofa women; I don't know as she'll ever get over it. And the other child's rather a mean cuss, I'm afraid. They love him the best. So I thought we'd educate Joan a bit.'

Joan's education was largely physical. A few weeks of free play, and then a few moments every day of the well-planned exercises Dr Warren had invented for his children. There were two ponies to ride; there were hills to climb; there was work to do in the well-irrigated garden. There were games, and I am obliged to confess, fights. Every one of those children was taught what we used to grandiloquently call 'the noble art of self-defense'; not only the skilled management of their hands, with swift 'footwork,' but the subtler methods of jiu-jitsu.

'I took the course on purpose,' the father explained to his friends, 'and the kids take to it like ducks to water.'

To her own great surprise, and her uncle's delight, Joan showed marked aptitude in her new studies. In the hours of definite instruction, from books or in nature study and laboratory work, she was happy and successful, but the rapture with which she learned to use her body was fine to see.

The lower reservoir made a good-sized swimming pool, and there she learned to float and dive. The big barn had a little simple apparatus for gymnastics in the rainy season, and the jolly companionship of all those bouncing cousins was an education in itself.

Dr Warren gave her special care, watched her food, saw to it that she was early put to bed on the wide sleeping porch, and trained her as carefully as if she had some tremendous contest before her. He trained her mind as well as her body. Those children were taught to reason, as well as to remember; taught to think for themselves, and to see through fallacious arguments. In body and mind she grew strong.

At first she whimpered a good deal when things hurt her, but finding that the other children did not, and that, though patient with her, they evidently disliked her doing it, she learned to take her share of the casualties of vigorous childhood without complaint.

At the end of the year Dr Warren wrote to his brother-in-law that it was not convenient for him to furnish the return ticket, or to take the trip himself, but if they could spare the child a while longer he would bring her back as agreed — that she was doing finely in all ways.

It was nearly two years when Joan Marsden, aged eleven, returned to her own home, a very different looking child from the one who left it so mournfully. She was much taller, larger, with a clear color, a light, firm step, a ready smile.

She greeted her father with no shadow of timidity, and rushed to her mother so eagerly as well-nigh to upset her.

'Why, child!' said the mother. 'Where's your beautiful hair? Arthur — how could you?'

'It is much better for her health,' he solemnly assured her. 'You see how much stronger she looks. Better keep it short till she's fourteen or fifteen.'

Gerald looked at his sister with mixed emotions. He had not grown as much. She was certainly as big as he was now. With her curls gone she was not so easy to hurt. However, there were other places. As an only child his disposition had not improved, and it was not long before that disposition led him to derisive remarks and then to personal annoyance, which increased as days passed.

She met him cheerfully. She met him patiently. She gave him fair warning. She sought to avoid his attacks, and withdrew herself to the far side of the garage, but he followed her.

'It's not fair, Gerald, and you know it,' said Joan. 'If you hurt me again I shall have to do something to you.'

'Oh you will, will you?' he jeered, much encouraged by her withdrawal, much amused by her threat. 'Let's see you do it — smarty! 'Fraid cat!' and he struck her again, a blow neatly planted, where the deltoid meets the biceps and the bone is near the surface.

Joan did not say, 'Now *stop*!' She did not whine, '*Please* don't!' She did not cry. She simply knocked him down.

And when he got up and rushed at her, furious, meaning to reduce this rebellious sister to her proper place, Joan set her teeth and gave him a clean thrashing.

'Will you give up?'

He did. He was glad to.

'Will you promise to behave? To let me alone?'

He promised.

She let him up, and even brushed off his dusty clothes.

'If you're mean to me any more, I'll do it again,' she said calmly. 'And if you want to tell mother — or father — or anybody — that I licked you, you may.'

But Gerald did not want to.

Three Thanksgivings

Andrew's letter and Jean's letter were in Mrs Morrison's lap. She had read them both, and sat looking at them with a varying sort of smile, now motherly and now unmotherly.

'You belong with me,' Andrew wrote. 'It is not right that Jean's husband should support my mother. I can do it easily now. You shall have a good room and every comfort. The old house will let for enough to give you quite a little income of your own, or it can be sold and I will invest the money where you'll get a deal more out of it. It is not right that you should live alone there. Sally is old and liable to accident. I am anxious about you. Come on for Thanksgiving — and come to stay. Here is the money to come with. You know I want you. Annie joins me in sending love. ANDREW.'

Mrs Morrison read it all through again, and laid it down with her quiet, twinkling smile. Then she read Jean's.

'Now, mother, you've got to come to us for Thanksgiving this year. Just think! You haven't seen baby since he was three months old! And have never seen the twins. You won't know him — he's such a splendid big boy now. Joe says for you to come, of course. And, mother, why won't you come and live with us? Joe wants you, too. There's the little room upstairs; it's not very big, but we can put in a Franklin stove for you and make you pretty comfortable. Joe says he should think you ought to sell that white elephant of a place. He says he could put the money into his store and pay you good interest. I wish you would, mother. We'd just love to have you here. You'd be such a comfort to me, and such a help with the babies. And Joe just loves you. Do come now, and stay with us. Here is the money for the trip. — Your affectionate daughter,

JEANNIE.'

Mrs Morrison laid this beside the other, folded both, and placed them in their respective envelopes, then in their several well-filled pigeon-holes in her big, old-fashioned desk. She turned and paced slowly up and down the long parlor, a tall woman, commanding of aspect, yet of a winningly attractive manner, erect and light-footed, still imposingly handsome.

It was now November, the last lingering boarder was long since gone, and a quiet winter lay before her. She was alone, but for Sally; and she smiled at Andrew's cautious expression, 'liable to accident.' He could not say 'feeble' or 'ailing,' Sally being a colored lady of changeless aspect and incessant activity.

Mrs Morrison was alone, and while living in the Welcome House she was never unhappy. Her father had built it, she was born there, she grew up playing on the broad green lawns in front, and in the acre of garden behind. It was the finest house in the village, and she then thought it the finest in the world.

Even after living with her father at Washington and abroad, after visiting hall, castle and palace, she still found the Welcome House beautiful and impressive.

If she kept on taking boarders she could live the year through, and pay interest, but not principal, on her little mortgage. This had been the one possible and necessary thing while the children were there, though it was a business she hated.

But her youthful experience in diplomatic circles, and the years of practical management in church affairs, enabled her to bear it with patience and success. The boarders often confided to one another, as they chatted and tatted on the long piazza, that Mrs Morrison was 'certainly very refined.'

Now Sally whisked in cheerfully, announcing supper, and Mrs Morrison went out to her great silver tea-tray at the lit end of the long, dark mahogany table, with as much dignity as if twenty titled guests were before her.

Afterward Mr Butts called. He came early in the evening, with his usual air of determination and a somewhat unusual spruceness. Mr Peter Butts was a florid, blond person, a little stout, a little pompous, sturdy and immovable in the attitude of a self-made man. He had been a poor boy when she was a rich girl; and it gratified him much to realize — and to call upon her to realize — that their positions had changed. He meant no unkindness, his pride was honest and unveiled. Tact he had none.

She had refused Mr Butts, almost with laughter, when he proposed to her in her gay girlhood. She had refused him, more gently, when he proposed to her in her early widowhood. He had always been her friend, and her husband's friend, a solid member of the church, and had taken the small mortgage on the house. She refused to allow him at first, but he was convincingly frank about it.

'This has nothing to do with my wanting you, Delia Morrison,' he said. 'I've always wanted you — and I've always wanted this house, too. You won't sell, but you've got to mortgage. By and by you can't pay up, and I'll get it — see? Then maybe you'll take me — to keep the house. Don't be a fool, Delia. It's a perfectly good investment.'

She had taken the loan. She had paid the interest. She would pay the interest if she had to take boarders all her life. And she would not, at any price, marry Peter Butts.

He broached the subject again that evening, cheerful and undismayed. 'You might as well come to it, Delia,' he said. 'Then, we could live right here just the same. You aren't so young as you were, to be sure; I'm not, either. But you are as good a housekeeper as ever — better — you've had more experience.'

'You are extremely kind, Mr Butts,' said the lady, 'but I do not wish to marry you.'

'I know you don't,' he said. 'You've made that clear. You don't, but I do. You've had your way and married the minister. He was a good man, but he's dead. Now you might as well marry me.'

'I do not wish to marry again, Mr Butts; neither you nor anyone.'

'Very proper, very proper, Delia,' he replied. 'It wouldn't look well if you did — at any rate, if you showed it. But why shouldn't you? The children are gone now — you can't hold them up against me any more.'

'Yes, the children are both settled now, and doing nicely,' she admitted.

'You don't want to go and live with them — either one of them — do you?' he asked.

'I should prefer to stay here,' she answered.

'Exactly! And you can't! You'd rather live here and be a grandee — but you can't do it. Keepin' house for boarders isn't any better than keepin' house for me, as I see. You'd much better marry me.'

'I should prefer to keep the house without you, Mr Butts.'

'I know you would. But you can't, I tell you. I'd like to know what a woman of your age can do with a house like this — and no money? You can't live eternally on hens' eggs and garden truck. That won't pay the mortgage.'

Mrs Morrison looked at him with her cordial smile, calm and non-committal. 'Perhaps I can manage it,' she said.

'That mortgage falls due two years from Thanksgiving, you know.'

'Yes — I have not forgotten.'

'Well, then, you might just as well marry me now, and save two years of interest. It'll be

204

my house, either way — but you'll be keepin' it just the same.'

'It is very kind of you, Mr Butts. I must decline the offer none the less. I can pay the interest, I am sure. And perhaps — in two years' time — I can pay the principal. It's not a large sum.'

'That depends on how you look at it,' said he. 'Two thousand dollars is considerable money for a single woman to raise in two years — *and* interest.'

He went away, as cheerful and determined as ever; and Mrs Morrison saw him go with a keen light in her fine eyes, a more definite line to that steady, pleasant smile.

Then she went to spend Thanksgiving with Andrew. He was glad to see her. Annie was glad to see her. They proudly installed her in 'her room,' and said she must call it 'home' now.

This affectionately offered home was twelve by fifteen, and eight feet high. It had two windows, one looking at some pale gray clapboards within reach of a broom, the other giving a view of several small fenced yards occupied by cats, clothes and children. There was an ailanthus tree under the window, a lady ailanthus tree. Annie told her how profusely it bloomed. Mrs Morrison particularly disliked the smell of ailanthus flowers. 'It doesn't bloom in November,' said she to herself. 'I can be thankful for that!'

Andrew's church was very like the church of his father, and Mrs Andrew was doing her best to fill the position of minister's wife — doing it well, too — there was no vacancy for a minister's mother.

Besides, the work she had done so cheerfully to help her husband was not what she most cared for, after all. She liked the people, she liked to manage, but she was not strong on doctrine. Even her husband had never known how far her views differed from his. Mrs Morrison had never mentioned what they were.

Andrew's people were very polite to her. She was invited out with them, waited upon and watched over and set down among the old ladies and gentlemen — she had never realized so keenly that she was no longer young. Here nothing recalled her youth, every careful provision anticipated age. Annie brought her a hot-water bag at night, tucking it in at the foot of the bed with affectionate care. Mrs Morrison thanked her, and subsequently took it out — airing the bed a little before she got into it. The house seemed very hot to her, after the big, windy halls at home.

The little dining-room, the little round

table with the little round fern-dish in the middle, the little turkey and the little carving-set — game-set she would have called it — all made her feel as if she was looking through the wrong end of an opera-glass.

In Annie's precise efficiency she saw no room for her assistance; no room in the church, no room in the small, busy town, prosperous and progressive, and no room in the house. 'Not enough to turn round in!' she said to herself. Annie, who had grown up in a city flat, thought their little parsonage palatial. Mrs Morrison grew up in the Welcome House.

She stayed a week, pleasant and polite, conversational, interested in all that went on.

'I think your mother is just lovely,' said Annie to Andrew.

'Charming woman, your mother,' said the leading church member.

'What a delightful old lady your mother is!' said the pretty soprano.

And Andrew was deeply hurt and disappointed when she announced her determination to stay on for the present in her old home. 'Dear boy,' she said, 'you mustn't take it to heart. I love to be with you, of course, but I love my home, and want to keep it as long as I can. It is a great pleasure to see you and Annie so well settled, and so happy together. I am most truly thankful for you.'

'My home is open to you whenever you wish to come, mother,' said Andrew. But he was a little angry.

Mrs Morrison came home as eager as a girl, and opened her own door with her own key, in spite of Sally's haste.

Two years were before her in which she must find some way to keep herself and Sally, and to pay two thousand dollars and the interest to Peter Butts. She considered her assets. Here was the house — the white elephant. It *was* big — very big. It was profusely furnished. Her father had entertained lavishly like the Southern-born, hospitable gentleman he was; and the bedrooms ran in suites — somewhat deteriorated by the use of boarders, but still numerous and habitable. Boarders — she abhorred them. They were people from afar, strangers and interlopers. She went over the place from garret to cellar, from front gate to backyard fence.

The garden had great possibilities. She was fond of gardening, and understood it well. She measured and estimated.

'This garden,' she finally decided, 'with the hens, will feed us two women and sell enough to pay Sally. If we make plenty of jelly, it may cover the coal bill, too. As to clothes — I don't need any. They last admirably. I can manage. I can *live* — but two thousand dollars — *and* interest!'

In the great attic was more furniture, discarded sets put there when her extravagant young mother had ordered new ones. And chairs — uncounted chairs. Senator Welcome used to invite numbers to meet his political friends — and they had delivered glowing orations in the wide, double parlors, the impassioned speakers standing on a temporary dais, now in the cellar; and the enthusiastic listeners disposed more or less comfortably on these serried rows of 'folding chairs,' which folded sometimes, and let down the visitor in scarlet confusion to the floor.

She sighed as she remembered those vivid days and glittering nights. She used to steal downstairs in her little pink wrapper and listen to the eloquence. It delighted her young soul to see her father rising on his toes, coming down sharply on his heels, hammering one hand upon the other; and then to hear the fusilade of applause.

Here were the chairs, often borrowed for weddings, funerals, and church affairs, somewhat worn and depleted, but still numerous. She mused upon them. Chairs — hundreds of chairs. They would sell for very little.

She went through her linen room. A

splendid stock in the old days; always carefully washed by Sally; surviving even the boarders. Plenty of bedding, plenty of towels, plenty of napkins and tablecloths. 'It would make a good hotel — but I *can't* have it so — I *can't*! Besides, there's no need of another hotel here. The poor little Haskins House is never full.'

The stock in the china closet was more damaged than some other things, naturally; but she inventoried it with care. The countless cups of crowded church receptions were especially prominent. Later additions these, not very costly cups, but numerous, appallingly.

When she had her long list of assets all in order, she sat and studied it with a clear and daring mind. Hotel — boarding-house — she could think of nothing else. School! A girls' school! A boarding school! There was money to be made at that, and fine work done. It was a brilliant thought at first, and she gave several hours, and much paper and ink, to its full consideration. But she would need some capital for advertising; she must engage teachers — adding to her definite obligation; and to establish it, well, it would require time.

Mr Butts, obstinate, pertinacious, oppressively affectionate, would give her no time. He meant to force her to marry him for her own good — and his. She shrugged her fine shoulders with a little shiver. Marry Peter Butts! Never! Mrs Morrison still loved her husband. Some day she meant to see him again — God willing — and she did not wish to have to tell him that at fifty she had been driven into marrying Peter Butts.

Better live with Andrew. Yet when she thought of living with Andrew, she shivered again. Pushing back her sheets of figures and lists of personal property, she rose to her full graceful height and began to walk the floor. There was plenty of floor to walk. She considered, with a set deep thoughtfulness, the town and the townspeople, the surrounding country, the hundreds upon hundreds of women whom she knew — and liked, and who liked her.

It used to be said of Senator Welcome that he had no enemies; and some people, strangers, maliciously disposed, thought it no credit to his character. His daughter had no enemies, but no one had ever blamed her for her unlimited friendliness. In her father's wholesale entertainments the whole town knew and admired his daughter; in her husband's popular church she had come to know the women of the countryside about them. Her mind strayed off to these women, farmers' wives, comfortably off in a plain way, but starving for companionship, for

211

occasional stimulus and pleasure. It was one of her joys in her husband's time to bring together these women — to teach and entertain them.

Suddenly she stopped short in the middle of the great high-ceiled room, and drew her head up proudly like a victorious queen. One wide, triumphant, sweeping glance she cast at the well-loved walls — and went back to her desk, working swiftly, excitedly, well into the hours of the night.

★　★　★

Presently the little town began to buzz, and the murmur ran far out into the surrounding country. Sunbonnets wagged over fences; butcher carts and pedlar's wagon carried the news farther; and ladies visiting found one topic in a thousand houses.

Mrs Morrison was going to entertain. Mrs Morrison had invited the whole feminine population, it would appear, to meet Mrs Isabelle Carter Blake, of Chicago. Even Haddleton had heard of Mrs Isabelle Carter Blake. And even Haddleton had nothing but admiration for her.

She was known the world over for her splendid work for children — for the school children and the working children of the

212

country. Yet she was known also to have lovingly and wisely reared six children of her own — and made her husband happy in his home. On top of that she had lately written a novel, a popular novel, of which everyone was talking; and on top of that she was an intimate friend of a certain conspicuous Countess — an Italian.

It was even rumored, by some who knew Mrs Morrison better than others — or thought they did — that the Countess was coming, too! No one had known before that Delia Welcome was a school-mate of Isabelle Carter, and a life-long friend; and that was ground for talk in itself.

The day arrived, and the guests arrived. They came in hundreds upon hundreds, and found ample room in the great white house.

The highest dream of the guests was realized — the Countess had come, too. With excited joy they met her, receiving impressions that would last them for all their lives, for those large widening waves of reminiscence which delight us the more as years pass. It was an incredible glory — Mrs Isabelle Carter Blake, *and* a Countess!

Some were moved to note that Mrs Morrison looked the easy peer of these eminent ladies, and treated the foreign nobility precisely as she did her other friends.

She spoke, her clear quiet voice reaching across the murmuring din, and silencing it.

'Shall we go into the east room? If you will all take chairs in the east room, Mrs Blake is going to be so kind as to address us. Also perhaps her friend — '

They crowded in, sitting somewhat timorously on the unfolded chairs.

Then the great Mrs Blake made them an address of memorable power and beauty, which received vivid sanction from that imposing presence in Parisian garments on the platform by her side. Mrs Blake spoke to them of the work she was interested in, and how it was aided everywhere by the women's clubs. She gave them the number of these clubs, and described with contagious enthusiasm the inspiration of their great meetings. She spoke of the women's club houses, going up in city after city, where many associations meet and help one another. She was winning and convincing and most entertaining — an extremely attractive speaker.

Had they a women's club there? They had not.

Not *yet*, she suggested, adding that it took no time at all to make one.

They were delighted and impressed with Mrs Blake's speech, but its effect was greatly intensified by the address of the Countess.

'I, too, am American,' she told them; 'born here, reared in England, married in Italy.' And she stirred their hearts with a vivid account of the women's clubs and associations all over Europe, and what they were accomplishing. She was going back soon, she said, the wiser and happier for this visit to her native land, and she should remember particularly this beautiful, quiet town, trusting that if she came to it again it would have joined the great sisterhood of women, 'whose hands were touching around the world for the common good.'

It was a great occasion.

The Countess left next day, but Mrs Blake remained, and spoke in some of the church meetings, to an ever widening circle of admirers. Her suggestions were practical.

'What you need here is a 'Rest and Improvement Club,'' she said. 'Here are all you women coming in from the country to do your shopping — and no place to go to. No place to lie down if you're tired, to meet a friend, to eat your lunch in peace, to do your hair. All you have to do is organize, pay some small regular due, and provide yourselves with what you want.'

There was a volume of questions and suggestions, a little opposition, much random activity.

Who was to do it? Where was there a suitable place? They would have to hire someone to take charge of it. It would only be used once a week. It would cost too much.

Mrs Blake, still practical, made another suggestion. 'Why not combine business with pleasure, and make use of the best place in town, if you can get it? I *think* Mrs Morrison could be persuaded to let you use part of her house; it's quite too big for one woman.'

Then Mrs Morrison, simple and cordial as ever, greeted with warm enthusiasm by her wide circle of friends.

'I have been thinking this over,' she said. 'Mrs Blake has been discussing it with me. My house is certainly big enough for all of you, and there am I, with nothing to do but entertain you. Suppose you formed such a club as you speak of — for Rest and Improvement. My parlors are big enough for all manner of meetings; there are bedrooms in plenty for resting. If you form such a club I shall be glad to help with my great, cumbersome house, shall be delighted to see so many friends there so often; and I think I could furnish accommodations more cheaply than you could manage in any other way.'

Then Mrs Blake gave them facts and figures, showing how much clubhouses cost — and how little this arrangement would cost. 'Most women have very little money, I know,' she said, 'and they hate to spend it on themselves when they have; but even a little money from each goes a long way when it is put together. I fancy there are none of us so poor we could not squeeze out, say ten cents a week. For a hundred women that would be ten dollars. Could you feed a hundred tired women for ten dollars, Mrs Morrison?'

Mrs Morrison smiled cordially. 'Not on chicken pie,' she said. 'But I could give them tea and coffee, crackers and cheese for that, I think. And a quiet place to rest, and a reading room, and a place to hold meetings.'

Then Mrs Blake quite swept them off their feet by her wit and eloquence. She gave them to understand that if a share in the palatial accommodation of the Welcome House, and as good tea and coffee as old Sally made, with a place to meet, a place to rest, a place to talk, a place to lie down, could be had for ten cents a week each, she advised them to clinch the arrangement at once before Mrs Morrison's natural good sense had overcome her enthusiasm.

Before Mrs Isabelle Carter Blake had left, Haddleton had a large and eager women's club, whose entire expenses, outside of stationery and postage, consisted of ten cents a week *per capita,* paid to Mrs Morrison.

Everybody belonged. It was open at once for charter members, and all pressed forward to claim that privileged place.

They joined by hundreds, and from each member came this tiny sum to Mrs Morrison each week. It was very little money, taken separately. But it added up with silent speed. Tea and coffee, purchased in bulk, crackers by the barrel, and whole cheeses — these are not expensive luxuries. The town was full of Mrs Morrison's ex-Sunday-school boys, who furnished her with the best they had — at cost. There was a good deal of work, a good deal of care, and room for the whole supply of Mrs Morrison's diplomatic talent and experience. Saturdays found the Welcome House as full as it could hold, and Sundays found Mrs Morrison in bed. But she liked it.

A busy, hopeful year flew by, and then she went to Jean's for Thanksgiving.

The room Jean gave her was about the same size as her haven in Andrew's home, but one flight higher up, and with a sloping ceiling. Mrs Morrison whitened her dark hair upon it, and rubbed her head confusedly. Then she shook it with renewed determination.

The house was full of babies. There was little Joe, able to get about, and into everything. There were the twins, and there was the new baby. There was one servant, over-worked and cross. There was a small, cheap, totally inadequate nursemaid. There was Jean, happy but tired, full of joy, anxiety and affection, proud of her children, proud of her husband, and delighted to unfold her heart to her mother.

By the hour she babbled of their cares and hopes, while Mrs Morrison, tall and elegant, in her well-kept old black silk, sat holding the baby or trying to hold the twins. The old silk was pretty well finished by the week's end. Joseph talked to her also, telling her how well he was getting on, and how much he needed capital, urging her to come and stay with them; it was such a help to Jeannie; asking questions about the house.

There was no going visiting here. Jeannie could not leave the babies. And few visitors; all the little suburb being full of similarly overburdened mothers. Such as called found Mrs Morrison charming. What she found them, she did not say. She bade her daughter an affectionate good-bye when the week was up, smiling at their mutual contentment.

'Good-bye, my dear children,' she said. 'I am so glad for all your happiness. I am thankful for both of you.'

But she was more thankful to get home.

Mr Butts did not have to call for his

interest this time, but he called none the less.

'How on earth'd you get it, Delia?' he demanded. 'Screwed it out o' these club-women?'

'Your interest is so moderate, Mr Butts, that it is easier to meet than you imagine,' was her answer. 'Do you know the average interest they charge in Colorado? The women vote there, you know.'

He went away with no more personal information than that; and no nearer approach to the twin goals of his desire than the passing of the year.

'One more year, Delia,' he said; 'then you'll have to give in.'

'One more year!' she said to herself, and took up her chosen task with renewed energy.

The financial basis of the undertaking was very simple, but it would never have worked so well under less skilful management. Five dollars a year these country women could not have faced, but ten cents a week was possible to the poorest. There was no difficulty in collecting, for they brought it themselves; no unpleasantness in receiving, for old Sally stood at the receipt of custom and presented the covered cash box when they came for their tea.

On the crowded Saturdays the great urns were set going, the mighty array of cups arranged in easy reach, the ladies filed by, each taking her refection and leaving her dime. Where the effort came was in enlarging the membership and keeping up the attendance; and this effort was precisely in the line of Mrs Morrison's splendid talents.

Serene, cheerful, inconspicuously active, planning like the born statesman she was, executing like a practical politician, Mrs Morrison gave her mind to the work, and thrived upon it. Circle within circle, and group within group, she set small classes and departments at work, having a boys' club by and by in the big room over the woodshed, girls' clubs, reading clubs, study clubs, little meetings of every sort that were not held in churches, and some that were — previously.

For each and all there was, if wanted, tea and coffee, crackers and cheese; simple fare, of unvarying excellence, and from each and all, into the little cashbox, ten cents for these refreshments. From the club members this came weekly; and the club members, kept up by a constant variety of interests, came every week. As to numbers, before the first six months was over The Haddleton Rest and Improvement Club numbered five hundred women.

Now, five hundred times ten cents a week is twenty-six hundred dollars a year. Twenty-six hundred dollars a year would not be very much to build or rent a large house, to furnish five hundred people with chairs, lounges, books and magazines, dishes and service; and with food and drink even of the simplest. But if you are miraculously supplied with a club-house, furnished, with a manager and servant on the spot, then that amount of money goes a long way.

On Saturdays Mrs Morrison hired two helpers for half a day, for half a dollar each. She stocked the library with many magazines for fifty dollars a year. She covered fuel, light, and small miscellanies with another hundred. And she fed her multitude with the plain viands agreed upon, at about four cents apiece.

For her collateral entertainments, her many visits, the various new expenses entailed, she paid as well; and yet at the end of the first year she had not only her interest, but a solid thousand dollars of clear profit. With a calm smile she surveyed it, heaped in neat stacks of bills in the small safe in the wall behind her bed. Even Sally did not know it was there.

The second season was better than the first. There were difficulties, excitements, even some opposition, but she rounded out the year triumphantly. 'After that,' she said to herself, 'they may have the deluge if they like.'

She made all expenses, made her interest, made a little extra cash, clearly her own, all over and above the second thousand dollars.

Then did she write to son and daughter, inviting them and their families to come home to Thanksgiving, and closing each letter with joyous pride: 'Here is the money to come with.'

They all came, with all the children and two nurses. There was plenty of room in the Welcome House, and plenty of food on the long mahogany table. Sally was as brisk as a bee, brilliant in scarlet and purple; Mrs Morrison carved her big turkey with queenly grace.

'I don't see that you're over-run with club women, mother,' said Jeannie.

'It's Thanksgiving, you know; they're all at home. I hope they are all as happy, as thankful for their homes as I am for mine,' said Mrs Morrison.

Afterward Mr Butts called. With dignity and calm unruffled, Mrs Morrison handed him his interest — and principal.

Mr Butts was almost loath to receive it, though his hand automatically grasped the crisp blue check.

'I didn't know you had a bank account,' he protested, somewhat dubiously.

'Oh, yes; you'll find the check will be

honored, Mr Butts.'

'I'd like to know how you got this money. You *can't* 'a' skinned it out o' that club of yours.'

'I appreciate your friendly interest, Mr Butts; you have been most kind.'

'I believe some of these great friends of yours have lent it to you. You won't be any better off, I can tell you.'

'Come, come, Mr Butts! Don't quarrel with good money. Let us part friends.'

And they parted.

Turned

In her soft-carpeted, thick-curtained, richly furnished chamber, Mrs Marroner lay sobbing on the wide, soft bed.

She sobbed bitterly, chokingly, despairingly; her shoulders heaved and shook convulsively; her hands were tight-clenched; she had forgotten her elaborate dress, the more elaborate bed-cover; forgotten her dignity, her self-control, her pride. In her mind was an overwhelming, unbelievable horror, an immeasurable loss, a turbulent, struggling mass of emotion.

In her reserved, superior, Boston-bred life she had never dreamed that it would be possible for her to feel so many things at once, and with such trampling intensity.

She tried to cool her feelings into thoughts; to stiffen them into words; to control herself — and could not. It brought vaguely to her mind an awful moment in the breakers at York Beach, one summer in girlhood, when she had been swimming under water and could not find the top.

★ ★ ★

In her uncarpeted, thin-curtained, poorly furnished chamber on the top floor, Gerta Petersen lay sobbing on the narrow, hard bed.

She was of larger frame than her mistress, grandly built and strong; but all her proud, young womanhood was prostrate now, convulsed with agony, dissolved in tears. She did not try to control herself. She wept for two.

★   ★   ★

If Mrs Marroner suffered more from the wreck and ruin of a longer love — perhaps a deeper one; if her tastes were finer, her ideals loftier; if she bore the pangs of bitter jealousy and outraged pride, Gerta had personal shame to meet, a hopeless future, and a looming present which filled her with unreasoning terror.

She had come like a meek young goddess into that perfectly ordered house, strong, beautiful, full of good will and eager obedience, but ignorant and childish — a girl of eighteen.

Mr Marroner had frankly admired her, and so had his wife. They discussed her visible perfections and as visible limitations with that perfect confidence which they had so long enjoyed. Mrs Marroner was not a jealous woman. She had never been jealous in her life — till now.

Gerta had stayed and learned their ways. They had both been fond of her. Even the cook was fond of her. She was what is called 'willing,' was unusually teachable and plastic; and Mrs Marroner, with her early habits of giving instruction, tried to educate her somewhat.

'I never saw anyone so docile,' Mrs Marroner had often commented. 'It is perfection in a servant, but almost a defect in character. She is so helpless and confiding.'

She was precisely that; a tall, rosy-cheeked baby; rich womanhood without, helpless infancy within. Her braided wealth of dead-gold hair, her grave blue eyes, her mighty shoulders, and long, firmly moulded limbs seemed those of a primal earth spirit; but she was only an ignorant child, with a child's weakness.

When Mr Marroner had to go abroad for his firm, unwillingly, hating to leave his wife, he had told her he felt quite safe to leave her in Gerta's hands — she would take care of her.

'Be good to your mistress, Gerta,' he told the girl that last morning at breakfast. 'I leave her to you to take care of. I shall be back in a month at latest.'

Then he turned, smiling, to his wife. 'And

you must take care of Gerta, too,' he said. 'I expect you'll have her ready for college when I get back.'

This was seven months ago. Business had delayed him from week to week, from month to month. He wrote to his wife, long, loving, frequent letters; deeply regretting the delay, explaining how necessary, how profitable it was; congratulating her on the wide resources she had; her well-filled, well-balanced mind; her many interests.

'If I should be eliminated from your scheme of things, by any of those 'acts of God' mentioned on the tickets, I do not feel that you would be an utter wreck,' he said. 'That is very comforting to me. Your life is so rich and wide that no one loss, even a great one, would wholly cripple you. But nothing of the sort is likely to happen, and I shall be home again in three weeks — if this thing gets settled. And you will be looking so lovely, with that eager light in your eyes and the changing flush I know so well — and love so well! My dear wife! We shall have to have a new honeymoon — other moons come every month, why shouldn't the mellifluous kind?'

He often asked after 'little Gerta,' sometimes enclosed a picture postcard to her, joked his wife about her laborious efforts to educate 'the child'; was so loving and merry and wise —

All this was racing through Mrs Marroner's mind as she lay there with the broad, hemstitched border of fine linen sheeting crushed and twisted in one hand, and the other holding a sodden handkerchief.

She had tried to teach Gerta, and had grown to love the patient, sweet-natured child, in spite of her dullness. At work with her hands, she was clever, if not quick, and could keep small accounts from week to week. But to the woman who held a Ph.D., who had been on the faculty of a college, it was like baby-tending.

Perhaps having no babies of her own made her love the big child the more, though the years between them were but fifteen.

To the girl she seemed quite old, of course; and her young heart was full of grateful affection for the patient care which made her feel so much at home in this new land.

And then she had noticed a shadow on the girl's bright face. She looked nervous, anxious, worried. When the bell rang she seemed startled, and would rush hurriedly to the door. Her peals of frank laughter no longer rose from the area gate as she stood talking with the always admiring tradesmen.

Mrs Marroner had labored long to teach

her more reserve with men, and flattered herself that her words were at last effective. She suspected the girl of homesickness; which was denied. She suspected her of illness, which was denied also. At last she suspected her of something which could not be denied.

For a long time she refused to believe it, waiting. Then she had to believe it, but schooled herself to patience and understanding. 'The poor child,' she said. 'She is here without a mother — she is so foolish and yielding — I must not be too stern with her.' And she tried to win the girl's confidence with wise, kind words.

But Gerta had literally thrown herself at her feet and begged her with streaming tears not to turn her away. She would admit nothing, explain nothing; but frantically promised to work for Mrs Marroner as long as she lived — if only she would keep her.

Revolving the problem carefully in her mind, Mrs Marroner thought she would keep her, at least for the present. She tried to repress her sense of ingratitude in one she had so sincerely tried to help, and the cold, contemptuous anger she had always felt for such weakness.

'The thing to do now,' she said to herself, 'is to see her through this safely. The child's life should not be hurt any more than is unavoidable. I will ask Dr Bleet about it — what a comfort a woman doctor is! I'll stand by the poor, foolish thing till it's over, and then get her back to Sweden somehow with her baby. How they do come where they are not wanted — and don't come where they are wanted!' And Mrs Marroner, sitting along in the quiet, spacious beauty of the house, almost envied Gerta.

Then came the deluge.

She had sent the girl out for needed air toward dark. The late mail came; she took it in herself. One letter for her — her husband's letter. She knew the postmark, the stamp, the kind of typewriting. She impulsively kissed it in the dim hall. No one would suspect Mrs Marroner of kissing her husband's letters — but she did, often.

She looked over the others. One was for Gerta, and not from Sweden. It looked precisely like her own. This struck her as a little odd, but Mr Marroner had several times sent messages and cards to the girl. She laid the letter on the hall table and took hers to her room.

'My poor child,' it began. What letter of hers had been sad enough to warrant that?

'I am deeply concerned at the news you send.' What news to so concern him had she written? 'You must bear it bravely, little girl. I shall be home soon, and will take care of you, of course. I hope there is no immediate anxiety — you do not say. Here is money, in case you need it. I expect to get home in a month at latest. If you have to go, be sure to leave your address at my office. Cheer up — be brave — I will take care of you.'

The letter was typewritten, which was not unusual. It was unsigned, which was unusual. It enclosed an American bill — fifty dollars. It did not seem in the least like any letter she had ever had from her husband, or any letter she could imagine him writing. But a strange, cold feeling was creeping over her, like a flood rising around a house.

She utterly refused to admit the ideas which began to bob and push about outside her mind, and to force themselves in. Yet under the pressure of these repudiated thoughts she went downstairs and brought up the other letter — the letter to Gerta. She laid them side by side on a smooth dark space on the table; marched to the piano and played, with stern precision, refusing to think, till the girl came back. When she came in, Mrs Marroner rose quietly and came to the table. 'Here is a letter for you,' she said.

The girl stepped forward eagerly, saw the two lying together there, hesitated, and looked at her mistress.

'Take yours, Gerta. Open it, please.'

The girl turned frightened eyes upon her.

'I want you to read it, here,' said Mrs Marroner.

'Oh, ma'am — No! Please don't make me!'

'Why not?'

There seemed to be no reason at hand, and Gerta flushed more deeply and opened her letter. It was long; it was evidently puzzling to her; it began 'My dear wife.' She read it slowly.

'Are you sure it is your letter?' asked Mrs Marroner. 'Is not this one yours? Is not that one — mine?'

She held out the other letter to her.

'It is a mistake,' Mrs Marroner went on, with a hard quietness. She had lost her social bearings somehow; lost her usual keen sense of the proper thing to do. This was not life, this was a nightmare.

'Do you not see? Your letter was put in my envelope and my letter was put in your envelope. Now we understand it.'

But poor Gerta had no antechamber to her mind; no trained forces to preserve order while agony entered. The thing swept over her, resistless, overwhelming. She cowered before the outraged wrath she expected; and from some hidden cavern that wrath arose and swept over her in pale flame.

'Go and pack your trunk,' said Mrs Marroner. 'You will leave my house to-night. Here is your money.'

She laid down the fifty-dollar bill. She put with it a month's wages. She had no shadow of pity for those anguished eyes, those tears which she heard drop on the floor.

'Go to your room and pack,' said Mrs Marroner. And Gerta, always obedient, went.

Then Mrs Marroner went to hers, and spent a time she never counted, lying on her face on the bed.

But the training of the twenty-eight years which had elapsed before her marriage; the life at college, both as student and teacher; the independent growth which she had made, formed a very different background for grief from that in Gerta's mind.

After a while Mrs Marroner arose. She administered to herself a hot bath, a cold shower, a vigorous rubbing. 'Now I can think,' she said.

First she regretted the sentence of instant banishment. She went upstairs to see if it had been carried out. Poor Gerta! The tempest of her agony had worked itself out at last as in a child, and left her sleeping, the pillow wet, the lips still grieving, a big sob shuddering itself off now and then.

Mrs Marroner stood and watched her, and

as she watched she considered the helpless sweetness of the face; the defenseless, unformed character; the docility and habit of obedience which made her so attractive — and so easily a victim. Also she thought of the mighty force which had swept over her; of the great process now working itself out through her; of how pitiful and futile seemed any resistance she might have made.

She softly returned to her own room, made up a little fire, and sat by it, ignoring her feelings now, as she had before ignored her thoughts.

Here were two women and a man. One woman was a wife; loving, trusting, affectionate. One was a servant; loving, trusting, affection-ate: a young girl, an exile, a dependent; grateful for any kindness; untrained, uneducated, child-ish. She ought, of course, to have resisted temptation; but Mrs Marroner was wise enough to know how difficult temptation is to recog-nize when it comes in the guise of friendship and from a source one does not suspect.

Gerta might have done better in resisting the grocer's clerk; had, indeed, with Mrs Marroner's advice, resisted several. But where respect was due, how could she criticize? Where obedience was due, how could she refuse — with ignorance to hold her blinded — until too late?

As the older, wiser woman forced herself to understand and extenuate the girl's misdeed and foresee her ruined future, a new feeling rose in her heart, strong, clear, and overmastering; a sense of measureless condemnation for the man who had done this thing. He knew. He understood. He could fully foresee and measure the consequences of his act. He appreciated to the full the innocence, the ignorance, the grateful affection, the habitual docility, of which he deliberately took advantage.

Mrs Marroner rose to icy peaks of intellectual apprehension, from which her hours of frantic pain seemed far indeed removed. He had done this thing under the same roof with her — his wife. He had not frankly loved the younger woman, broken with his wife, made a new marriage. That would have been heart-break pure and simple. This was something else.

That letter, that wretched, cold, carefully guarded, unsigned letter: that bill — far safer than a check — these did not speak of affection. Some men can love two women at one time. This was not love.

Mrs Marroner's sense of pity and outrage for herself, the wife, now spread suddenly into a perception of pity and outrage for the girl. All that splendid, clean young beauty, the hope of a happy life, with marriage and motherhood; honorable independence, even — these were nothing to that man. For his own pleasure he had chosen to rob her of her life's best joys.

He would 'take care of her' said the letter? How? In what capacity?

And then, sweeping over both her feelings for herself, the wife, and Gerta, his victim, came a new flood, which literally lifted her to her feet. She rose and walked, her head held high. 'This is the sin of man against woman,' she said. 'The offense is against womanhood. Against motherhood. Against — the child.'

She stopped.

The child. His child. That, too, he sacrificed and injured — doomed to degradation.

Mrs Marroner came of stern New England stock. She was not a Calvinist, hardly even a Unitarian, but the iron of Calvinism was in her soul: of that grim faith which held that most people had to be damned 'for the glory of God.'

Generations of ancestors who both preached and practiced stood behind her; people whose lives had been sternly moulded to their highest moments of religious conviction. In sweeping bursts of feeling they achieved 'conviction,' and afterward they lived and died according to that conviction.

When Mr Marroner reached home, a few weeks later, following his letters too soon to expect an answer to either, he saw no wife upon the pier, though he had cabled; and found the house closed darkly. He let himself in with his latch-key, and stole softly upstairs, to surprise his wife.

No wife was there.

He rang the bell. No servant answered it.

He turned up light after light; searched the house from top to bottom; it was utterly empty. The kitchen wore a clean, bald, unsympathetic aspect. He left it and slowly mounted the stair, completely dazed. The whole house was clean, in perfect order, wholly vacant.

One thing he felt perfectly sure of — she knew.

Yet was he sure? He must not assume too much. She might have been ill. She might have died. He started to his feet. No, they would have cabled him. He sat down again.

For any such change, if she had wanted him to know, she would have written. Perhaps she had, and he, returning so suddenly, had missed the letter. The thought was some comfort. It must be so. He turned to the telephone, and again hesitated. If she had found out — if she had gone — utterly gone, without a word — should he announce it

240

himself to friends and family?

He walked the floor; he searched everywhere for some letter, some word of
explanation. Again and again he went to the
telephone — and always stopped. He could
not bear to ask: 'Do you know where my wife
is?'

The harmonious, beautiful rooms reminded
him in a dumb, helpless way of her; like the
remote smile on the face of the dead. He put
out the lights; could not bear the darkness;
turned them all on again.

It was a long night —

In the morning he went early to the office.
In the accumulated mail was no letter from
her. No one seemed to know of anything
unusual. A friend asked after his wife — 'Pretty
glad to see you, I guess?' He answered evasively.

About eleven a man came to see him;
John Hill, her lawyer. Her cousin, too. Mr
Marroner had never liked him. He liked him
less now, for Mr Hill merely handed him a
letter, remarked, 'I was requested to deliver
this to you personally,' and departed, looking
like a person who is called on to kill
something offensive.

'I have gone. I will care for Gerta.
Good-bye. Marion.'

That was all. There was no date, no
address, no postmark; nothing but that.

In his anxiety and distress he had fairly forgotten Gerta and all that. Her name aroused in him a sense of rage. She had come between him and his wife. She had taken his wife from him. That was the way he felt.

At first he said nothing, did nothing; lived on alone in his house, taking meals where he chose. When people asked him about his wife he said she was traveling — for her health. He would not have it in the newspapers. Then, as time passed, as no enlightenment came to him, he resolved not to bear it any longer, and employed detectives. They blamed him for not having put them on the track earlier, but set to work, urged to the utmost secrecy.

What to him had been so blank a wall of mystery seemed not to embarrass them in the least. They made careful inquiries as to her 'past,' found where she had studied, where taught, and on what lines; that she had some little money of her own, that her doctor was Josephine L. Bleet, M.D., and many other bits of information.

As a result of careful and prolonged work, they finally told him that she had resumed teaching under one of her old professors; lived quietly, and apparently kept boarders; giving him town, street, and number, as if it were a matter of no difficulty whatever.

He had returned in early spring. It was

autumn before he found her.

A quiet college town in the hills, a broad, shady street, a pleasant house standing in its own lawn, with trees and flowers about it. He had the address in his hand, and the number showed clear on the white gate. He walked up the straight gravel path and rang the bell. An elderly servant opened the door.

'Does Mrs Marroner live here?'

'No, sir.'

'This is number twenty-eight?'

'Yes, sir.'

'Who does live here?'

'Miss Wheeling, sir.'

Ah! Her maiden name. They had told him, but he had forgotten.

He stepped inside. 'I would like to see her,' he said.

He was ushered into a still parlor, cool and sweet with the scent of flowers, the flowers she had always loved best. It almost brought tears to his eyes. All their years of happiness rose in his mind again; the exquisite beginnings; the days of eager longing before she was really his; the deep, still beauty of her love.

Surely she would forgive him — she must forgive him. He would humble himself; he would tell her of his honest remorse — his absolute determination to be a different man.

Through the wide doorway there came in to him two women. One like a tall Madonna, bearing a baby in her arms.

Marion, calm, steady, definitely impersonal; nothing but a clear pallor to hint of inner stress.

Gerta, holding the child as a bulwark, with a new intelligence in her face, and her blue, adoring eyes fixed on her friend — not upon him.

He looked from one to the other dumbly.

And the woman who had been his wife asked quietly:

'What have you to say to us?'

A Council of War

There was an informal meeting of women in a London drawing room, a meeting not over large, between twenty and thirty, perhaps, but of a deadly earnestness. Picked women were these, true and tried, many wearing the broad arrow pin, that badge of shame now turned to honor by sheer heroism. Some would qualify this as 'blind' heroism or 'senseless' heroism. But then, heroes have never been distinguished by a cautious farsightedness or a canny common sense.

No one, not even a one-ideaed physician, could call these women hysterical or morbid. On the contrary they wore a look of calm, uncompromising determination, and were vigorous and healthy enough, save indeed those who had been in prison, and one rather weazened working woman from the north. Still, no one had ever criticized the appearance of the working women, or called them hysterical, as long as they merely worked.

They had been recounting the measures taken in the last seven years, with their results, and though there was no sign of weakening in any face, neither was there any lively hope.

247

'It is the only way,' said one, a slender pretty woman of over forty, who looked like a girl. 'We've just got to keep it up, that's all.'

'I'm willing enough,' said one who wore the arrow badge, speaking with slow determination. Her courage was proved, and her endurance. 'I'm *willing* — but we've got to be dead certain that it's really the best way.'

'It's the only way!' — protested Lady Horditch, a tall gentle earnest woman, with a pink face and quiet voice.

'They'll ruin us all — they're after the money now.' This from a woman who had none of her own.

'They'll simply kill our leaders — one after another.' One of the working women said that with a break in her voice. She could not lead, but she could follow — to the very end.

'One thing we have done, anyhow — we've forced their hand,' suggested Mrs Shortham, a pleasant matronly woman who had been most happily married, the mother of a large and fine family, now all grown and established — 'we've made the men say what they really think of us — what they've really thought all the time — only they hid it — owing to chivalry.'

'Another thing is that we've brought out the real men — the best ones — we know our friends from our enemies now,' said a clear eyed girl.

'It begins to look like war — in this country, at least,' Lady Horwich remarked.

Little Mrs Wedge suggested:

'It's a sort of strike, *I* think — begging your Ladyship's pardon. They're willing to have us — and use us — on their own terms. But we're on strike now — that's what we are! We're striking for shorter hours,' — she laughed a grim little laugh, intelligent smiles agreed with her, 'and for higher wages, and for' there was a catch in her breath as she looked around at them — 'for the Union!'

'Ah!' — and a deep breath all around, a warm handclasp from Lady Horditch who sat next to her, 'Hear, Hear!' from several.

Miss Waltress, a sturdy attractive blonde woman of about thirty, well-known for her highly popular love stories, had been sitting quite silent so far, listening to every word. Now she lifted her head.

'When men began to strike they were in small groups — fiercely earnest, but small and therefore weak. They were frequently violent. They were usually beaten on legal grounds, because of their violence; they were supplemented by others who took their places, or they were starved out — because of their poverty. Why do they so frequently succeed now?'

She looked at Mrs Wedge from Lancashire,

and Mrs Wedge looked back at her with a kindling eye.

'Because there's so many of 'em now — and they hang together so well, and they keep on the safe side of the law, *and* they've got the brass.'

Miss Walters nodded. 'Exactly,' said she. 'Now friends, I've got something to suggest to you, something very earnest. Mrs Shortham and I have been talking about it for days, — she has something to say first.'

'I think it comes with as good grace from me as from anybody,' that lady began quietly. 'All of you know how absolutely happy I was with one of the best men God ever made. That shows I'm not prejudiced. And it can't hurt his feelings, now. As to his 'memory' — he put me up to most of this, and urged me to publish it — but I — I just *couldn't* while he was alive.'

Most of them had known Hugh Shortham, a tall deep-chested jovial man, always one of the most ardent advocates of the enlargement of women. His big manliness, his efficiency and success, had always made him a tower of strength against those who still talk of 'short-haired women and long-haired men' as the sole supporters of this cause.

What Mrs Shortham now read was a brief but terrible indictment of what the title called

'The Human Error.' It recounted the evil results of male rule, as affecting the health, beauty, intelligence, prosperity, progress and happiness of humanity, in such clear and terrible terms, with such an accumulating pile of injuries, that faces grew white and lips set in hard steely lines as they listened.

'All this does not in the least militate against the beauty and use of true manhood in right relation to women, nor does it contradict the present superior development of men in all lines of social progress. It does, however, in some sort make out the case against man. There follows the natural corollary that we, the women of to-day, seeing these things, must with all speed possible set ourselves to remove this devastating error in relation, and to establish a free and conscious womanhood for the right service of the world.'

There was a hot silence, with little murmurs of horror at some of the charges she had made, and a stir of new determination. Not all of them, keen as they were for the ballot, deeply as they felt the unnecessary sorrows of women, had ever had the historic panorama of injustice and its deadly consequences so vividly set before them.

'I knew it was bad enough,' broke forth little Mrs Wedge, 'but I never knew it was as bad as *that*. Look at the consequences.'

251

'That's exactly it, Mrs Wedge! It's the consequences we are looking at. We are tired of these consequences. We want some new ones!' and Miss Waltress looked around the room, from face to face.

'I'm ready!' said a pale thin woman with an arrow pin.

They were, every one of them. Then Miss Waltress began.

'What I have to suggest, is a wider, deeper, longer, stronger strike.'

Mrs Wedge, her eyes fixed on the calm earnest face, drew in her breath with a big intake.

'Even if we get the ballot in a year — the work is only begun. Men have had that weapon for a good while now, and they have not accomplished everything — even for themselves. And if we do not get it in a year — or five — or ten — are we to do nothing in all that time save repeat what we have done before? I know the ballot is the best weapon, but — there are others. There are enough of us to keep up our previous tactics as long as we hold it necessary. I say nothing whatever against it. But there are also enough of us to be doing other things too.

'Here is my suggestion. We need a government within a government; an organization of women, growing and strengthening against the time when it may come forward in full equality with that of men; a training school for world politics. This may become a world-group, holding international meetings and influencing the largest issues. I speak here only of a definite, practical beginning in this country.

'Let us form a committee, called, perhaps, 'Advisory Committee on Special Measures,' or simpler still, we might call it 'Extension Committee' — that tells nothing, and has no limitations.

'The measures I propose are these: —

'That we begin a series of business undertakings, plain ordinary, every day businesses — farms, market gardens, greenhouses, small fruits, preserves, confections, bakeries, eating-houses, boarding and lodging houses, hotels, milliners and dressmakers' shops, laundries, schools, kindergartens, nurseries — any and every business which women can enter.

'Yes, I know that women are in these things now, — but they are not united, not organized. This is a great spreading league of interconnected businesses, with the economic advantages of such large union.'

'Like a trust,' said Mrs Shortham. 'A woman's trust.'

'Or a Co-operative Society — or a Friendly,' breathed little Mrs Wedge, her cheeks flushing.

'Yes, all this and more. This is no haphazard solitary struggle of isolated women, competing with men, this is a body of women that can grow to an unlimited extent, and be stronger and richer as it grows. But it can begin as small as you please, and without any noise whatever.

'Now see here — you all know how women are sweated and exploited; how they overwork us and underpay us, and how they try to keep us out of trades and professions just as the Americans try to keep out Chinese labor — because they are afraid of being driven out of the market by a lower standard of living.

'Very well. Suppose we take them on their own terms. *Because* we can live on nothing a week and find ourselves — therefore we can cut the ground out from under their feet!'

The bitter intensity of her tones made a little shiver run around the circle, but they all shared her feeling.

'Don't imagine I mean to take over the business of the world — by no means. But I mean to initiate a movement which means on the surface, in immediate results, only some women going into business — that's no novelty! Underneath it means a great growing association with steady increase of power.'

'To what end — as a war measure, I mean?' Lady Horwich inquired.

'To several ends. The most patent, perhaps, is to accumulate the sinews of war. The next is to become owners of halls to speak in, of printing and publishing offices, of paper mills perhaps, of more and more of the necessary machinery needed for our campaign. The third is to train more and more women in economic organization, in the simple daily practice of modern business methods, and to guarantee to more and more of them that foundation stone of all other progress, economic independence. The fourth is to establish in all these businesses as we take them up, *right conditions* — proper hours, proper wages, everything as it should be.'

'Employing women, only?'

'As far as possible, Mrs Wedge. And when men are needed, employing the right kind.'

There was a thoughtful silence.

'It's an ENORMOUS undertaking,' murmured the Honorable Miss Erwood, a rather grim faced spinster of middle age. 'How can you get 'em to do it?'

Miss Waltress met her cheerfully.

'It is enormous, but natural. It does not require a million women to start at once you see; or any unusual undertaking. The advisory central committee will keep books and make plans. Each business, little or big, starts wherever it happens to be needed. The connection is not visible. That connection involves in the first place definite help and patronage in starting, or in increasing the custom of one already started; second, an advantage in buying — which will increase as the allied businesses increase; and then the paying to the central committee of a small annual fee. As the membership increases, all these advantages increase — in arithmetical progression.'

'Is the patronage in your plan confined to our society? Or to sympathizers?' pursued Miss Erwood.

'By no means. The very essence of the scheme is to meet general demands to prove the advantage of clean, honest efficiency.

'Now, for instance — ' Miss Waltress turned over a few notes she held in a neat package — 'here is — let us say — the necktie trade. Now neckties are not laborious to make — as a matter of fact women do make them to-day. Neckties are not difficult to sell. As a matter of fact women frequently sell them. Silk itself was first made use of by a woman, and the whole silk industry might be largely in their hands. Designing, spinning, weaving, dyeing, we might do it all. But in the mere matters of making and selling the present day necktie of mankind, there is absolutely nothing to prevent our stretching out a slow soft hand, and gathering in the business. We might begin in the usual spectacular 'feminine' way. A dainty shop in a good street, some fine girls, level-headed ones, who are working for the cause, to sell neckties, or — here is an advertising suggestion — we might call it 'The Widows' Shop' and employ only widows. There are always enough of the poor things needing employment.

'Anyhow we establish a trade in neckties, fine neckties, good taste, excellent materials, reliable workmanship. When it is sufficiently prosperous, it branches — both in town and in the provinces — little by little we could build up such a reputation that 'Widow Shop Neckties' would have a definite market value the world over. Meanwhile we could have our own workrooms, regular show places — patrons could see the neckties made, short hours, good wages, low prices.'

She was a little breathless, but very eager. 'Now I know you are asking how we are going to make all these things *pay*, for they must, if we are to succeed. You see, in ordinary business each one preys on the others. We propose to have an interconnected group that will help one another — that is where the profit comes. This was only a single instance, just one industry, but now I'll outline a group. Suppose we have a bit of land in some part of the country that is good for small fruit raising, and we study and develop that industry to its best. For the product we open a special shop in town, or at first, perhaps getting patronage by circularizing among our present membership, but winning our market by the goodness of the product and the reasonable price. Then we have a clean, pretty, scientific preserving room, and every bit of the unsold fruit is promptly turned into jam or jelly or syrup, right in sight of the patrons. They can see it done — and take it home, 'hot' if they wish to, or mark the jars and have them sent. That would be a legitimate beginning of a business that has practically no limits — and if it isn't a woman's business, I don't know what is!

'Now this could get a big backing of steady orders from boarding houses and hotels managed by women, and gradually more and more of these would be run by our own members. Then we could begin to effect a combination with Summer lodgings — think what missionary work it would be to establish a perfect chain of Summer boarding houses which should be as near perfect as is humanly possible, and all play into one another's hands and into our small market garden local ventures.

'On such a chain of hotels we could found a growing laundry business. In connection

258

with the service required, we could open an Employment Agency; in connection with that a Training School for Modern Employees — not 'slaveys,' to be 'exploited' by the average household, but swift, accurate, efficient, self-respecting young women, unionized and working for our own patrons. That would lead to club-houses for these girls — and for other working girls; and step by step, as the circles widened, we should command a market for our own produce that would be a tremendous business asset.'

She paused, looking about her, eager and flushed. Mrs Shortham took up the tale in her calm, sweet voice.

'You see how it opens,' she said. 'Beginning with simple practical local affairs — a little laundry here, a little bakeshop there; a fruit garden — honey, vegetables — what you like; with dressmakers and milliners and the rest. It carries certain definite advantages from the start; good conditions, wages, hours; and its range of possible growth is quite beyond our calculations. And it requires practically no capital. We have simply to plan, to create, to arrange, and the pledged patronage of say a thousand women of those now interested would mean backing enough to start any modest business.'

'There are women among us who have

money enough to make several beginnings,' Lady Horwich suggested.

'There'll be no trouble about that — we have to be sure of the working plan, that's all,' Miss Erwood agreed.

'There's a-plenty of us workers that could put it through — with good will!' Mrs Wedge confidently asserted. 'We're doing most of this work you speak of now, with cruel hours and a dog's wages. This offers a job to a woman with everything better than she had before — you'll have no trouble with the workers.'

'But how about the funds? — there might be a great deal of money in time,' suggested Mrs Doughton-Highbridge. 'Who would handle it?'

'There would have to be a financial committee of our very best — names we all know and trust; and then the whole thing should be kept open and above board, as far as possible.

'There should be certain small return benefits — that would attract many; a steady increase in the business, and a 'war chest' — the reserve power to meet emergencies.'

'I don't quite see how it would help us to get the ballot,' one earnest young listener now remarked, and quiet Mrs Shortham answered out of a full heart.

'Oh, my dear! Don't you see? In the mere matter of funds and membership it will help. In the very practical question of public opinion it will help; success in a work of this sort carries conviction with it. It will help as an immense machine for propaganda — all the growing numbers of our employees and fellow-members, all these shops and their spreading patronage. It will help directly as soon as we can own some sort of hall to speak in, in all large towns, and our own publishing house and printing shop. And while we are waiting and working and fighting for the ballot, this would be improving life for more and more women all the time.'

'And it would carry the proof that the good things we want done are practical and *can* be done — it would promote all good legislation,' Miss Waltress added.

'I see; it's all a practical good thing from the start,' said Miss Erwood, rather argumentatively. 'To begin with, it's just plain good work. Furnishes employment and improves conditions. And from that up, there is no top to it — it's education and organization, widening good fellowship and increasing power — I'm for it definitely.'

'It would be a world within a world — ready to come out full-grown a woman's world, clean and kind and safe and serviceable,' Lady Horwich murmured, as if to herself. 'Ladies, I move that a committee be appointed forthwith, consisting of Mrs Shortham, Mrs Wedge and Miss Waltress, with power to consult as widely as they see fit, and to report further as to this proposition at our next meeting.'

The motion was promptly seconded, as promptly carried, and the women looked at one another with the light of a new hope in their eyes.

Mr Peeble's Heart

He was lying on the sofa in the homely, bare little sitting room; an uncomfortable stiff sofa, too short, too sharply upcurved at the end, but still a sofa, whereon one could, at a pinch, sleep.

Thereon Mr Peebles slept, this hot still afternoon; slept uneasily, snoring a little, and twitching now and then, as one in some obscure distress.

Mrs Peebles had creaked down the front stairs and gone off on some superior errands of her own; with a good palm-leaf fan for a weapon, a silk umbrella for a defense.

'Why don't you come too, Joan?' she had urged her sister, as she dressed herself for departure.

'Why should I, Emma? It's much more comfortable at home. I'll keep Arthur company when he wakes up.'

'Oh, Arthur! He'll go back to the store as soon as he's had his nap. And I'm sure Mrs Older's paper'll be real interesting. If you're going to live here you ought to take an interest in the club, seems to me.'

'I'm going to live here as a doctor — not as

a lady of leisure, Em. You go on — I'm contented.'

So Mrs Emma Peebles sat in the circle of the Ellsworth Ladies' Home Club, and improved her mind, while Dr J. R. Bascom softly descended to the sitting room in search of a book she had been reading.

There was Mr Peebles, still uneasily asleep. She sat down quietly in a cane-seated rocker by the window and watched him awhile; first professionally, then with a deeper human interest.

Baldish, grayish, stoutish, with a face that wore a friendly smile for customers, and showed grave, set lines that deepened about the corners of his mouth when there was no one to serve; very ordinary in dress, in carriage, in appearance was Arthur Peebles at fifty. He was not 'the slave of love' of the Arab tale, but the slave of duty.

If ever a man had done his duty — as he saw it — he had done his, always.

His duty — as he saw it — was carrying women. First his mother, a comfortable competent person, who had run the farm after her husband's death, and added to their income by Summer boarders until Arthur was old enough to 'support her.' Then she sold the old place and moved into the village to 'make a home for Arthur,' who incidentally provided a hired girl to perform the manual labor of that process.

He worked in the store. She sat on the piazza and chatted with her neighbors.

He took care of his mother until he was nearly thirty, when she left him finally; and then he installed another woman to make a home for him — also with the help of the hired girl. A pretty, careless, clinging little person he married, who had long made mute appeal to his strength and carefulness, and she had continued to cling uninterruptedly to this day.

Incidentally a sister had clung until she married, another until she died; and his children — two daughters, had clung also. Both the daughters were married in due time, with sturdy young husbands to cling to in their turn; and now there remained only his wife to carry, a lighter load than he had ever known — at least numerically.

But either he was tired, very tired, or Mrs Peebles' tendrils had grown tougher, tighter, more tenacious, with age. He did not complain of it. Never had it occurred to him in all these years that there was any other thing for a man to do than to carry whatsoever women came within range of lawful relationship.

Had Dr Joan been — shall we say

— carriageable — he would have cheerfully added her to the list, for he liked her extremely. She was different from any woman he had ever known, different from her sister as day from night, and, in lesser degree, from all the female inhabitants of Ellsworth.

She had left home at an early age, against her mother's will, absolutely ran away; but when the whole countryside rocked with gossip and sought for the guilty man — it appeared that she had merely gone to college. She worked her way through, learning more, far more, than was taught in the curriculum; became a trained nurse, studied medicine, and had long since made good in her profession. There were even rumors that she must be 'pretty well fixed' and about to 'retire'; but others held that she must have failed, really or she never would have come back home to settle.

Whatever the reason, she was there, a welcome visitor; a source of real pride to her sister, and of indefinable satisfaction to her brother-in-law. In her friendly atmosphere he felt a stirring of long unused powers; he remembered funny stories, and how to tell them; he felt a revival of interests he had thought quite outlived, early interests in the big world's movements.

'Of all unimpressive, unattractive, *good* little men — ' she was thinking, as she watched, when one of his arms dropped off the slippery side of the sofa, the hand thumped on the floor, and he awoke and sat up hastily with an air of one caught off duty.

'Don't sit up as suddenly as that, Arthur, it's bad for your heart.'

'Nothing the matter with my heart, is there?' he asked with his ready smile.

'I don't know — haven't examined it. Now — sit still — you know there's nobody in the store this afternoon — and if there is, Jake can attend to 'em.'

'Where's Emma?'

'Oh, Emma's gone to her 'club' or something — wanted me to go, but I'd rather talk with you.'

He looked pleased but incredulous, having a high opinion of that club, and a low one of himself.

'Look here,' she pursued suddenly, after he had made himself comfortable with a drink from the swinging ice-pitcher, and another big cane rocker, 'what would you like to do if you could?'

'Travel!' said Mr Peebles, with equal suddenness. He saw her astonishment. 'Yes, travel! I've always wanted to — since I was a kid. No use! We never could, you see. And now — even if we could — Emma hates it.' He sighed resignedly

'Do you like to keep store?' she asked sharply.

'*Like* it?' He smiled at her cheerfully, bravely, but with a queer blank hopeless background underneath. He shook his head gravely. 'No, I do not, Joan. Not a little bit. But what of that?'

They were still for a little, and then she put another question. 'What would you have chosen — for a profession — if you had been free to choose?'

His answer amazed her threefold; from its character, its sharp promptness, its deep feeling. It was in one word — 'Music!'

'Music!' she repeated. 'Music! Why I didn't know you played — or cared about it.'

'When I was a youngster,' he told her, his eyes looking far off through the vine-shaded window, 'father brought home a guitar — and said it was for the one that learned to play it first. He meant the girls of course. As a matter of fact I learned it first — but I didn't get it. That's all the music I ever had,' he added. 'And there's not much to listen to here, unless you count what's in church. I'd have a Victrola — but — ' he laughed a little shamefacedly, 'Emma says if I bring one into the house she'll smash it. She says they're worse than cats. Tastes differ you know, Joan.'

Again he smiled at her, a droll smile, a little pinched at the corners. 'Well — I must be

270

getting back to business.'

She let him go, and turned her attention to her own business, with some seriousness.

'Emma,' she proposed, a day or two later. 'How would you like it if I should board here — live here, I mean, right along.'

'I should hope you would,' her sister replied. 'It would look nice to have you practising in this town and not live with me — all the sister I've got.'

'Do you think Arthur would like it?'

'Of course he would! Besides — even if he didn't — you're *my* sister — and this is my house. He put it in my name, long ago.'

'I see,' said Joan, 'I see.'

Then after a little — 'Emma — are you contented?'

'Contented? Why, of course I am. It would be a sin not to be. The girls are well married — I'm happy about them both. This is a real comfortable house, and it runs itself — my Matilda is a jewel if ever there was one. And she don't mind company — likes to do for 'em. Yes — I've nothing to worry about.'

'Your health's good — that I can see,' her sister remarked, regarding with approval her clear complexion and bright eyes.

'Yes — I've nothing to complain about — that I know of,' Emma admitted, but among her causes for thankfulness she did not even mention Arthur, nor seem to think of him till Dr Joan seriously inquired her opinion as to his state of health.

'His health? Arthur's? Why he's always well. Never had a sick day in his life — except now and then he's had a kind of a breakdown,' she added as an afterthought.

Dr Joan Bascom made acquaintances in the little town, both professional and social. She entered upon her practise, taking it over from the failing hands of old Dr Braithwaite — her first friend, and feeling very much at home in the old place. Her sister's house furnished two comfortable rooms downstairs, and a large bedroom above. 'There's plenty of room now the girls are gone,' they both assured her.

Then, safely ensconced and established, Dr Joan began a secret campaign to alienate the affections of her brother-in law. Not for herself — oh no! If ever in earlier years she had felt the need of some one to cling to, it was long, long ago. What she sought was to free him from the tentacles — without reentanglement.

She bought a noble gramophone with a set of first-class records, told her sister smilingly that she didn't have to listen, and Emma would sit sulkily in the back room on the other side of the house, while her husband

and sister enjoyed the music. She grew used to it in time, she said, and drew nearer, sitting on the porch perhaps; but Arthur had his long denied pleasure in peace.

It seemed to stir him strangely. He would rise and walk, a new fire in his eyes, a new firmness about the patient mouth, and Dr Joan fed the fire with talk and books and pictures with study of maps and sailing lists and accounts of economical tours.

'I don't see what you two find so interesting in all that stuff about music and those composers,' Emma would say. 'I never did care for foreign parts — musicians are all foreigners, anyway.'

Arthur never quarrelled with her; he only grew quiet and lost that interested sparkle of the eye when she discussed the subject.

Then one day, Mrs Peebles being once more at her club, content and yet aspiring, Dr Joan made bold attack upon her brother-in-law's principles.

'Arthur,' she said. 'Have you confidence in me as a physician?'

'I have,' he said briskly. 'Rather consult you than any doctor I ever saw.'

'Will you let me prescribe for you if I tell you you need it?'

'I sure will.'

'Will you take the prescription?'

'Of course I'll take it — no matter how it tastes.'

'Very well. I prescribe two years in Europe.'

He stared at her, startled.

'I mean it. You're in a more serious condition than you think. I want you to cut clear — and travel. For two years.'

He still stared at her. 'But Emma — '

'Never mind about Emma. She owns the house. She's got enough money to clothe herself — and I'm paying enough board to keep everything going. Emma don't need you.'

'But the store — '

'Sell the store.'

'Sell it! That's easy said. Who'll buy it?'

'I will. Yes — I mean it. You give me easy terms and I'll take the store off your hands. It ought to be worth seven or eight thousand dollars, oughtn't it — stock and all?'

He assented, dumbly.

'Well, I'll buy it. You can live abroad for two years, on a couple of thousand, or twenty-five hundred — a man of your tastes. You know those accounts we've read — it can be done easily. Then you'll have five thousand or so to come back to — and can invest it in something better than that shop. Will you do it — ?'

He was full of protests, of impossibilities.

She met them firmly. 'Nonsense! You can

too. She doesn't need you, at all — she may later. No — the girls don't need you — and they may later. Now is your time — *now*. They say the Japanese sow their wild oats after they're fifty — suppose you do! You can't be so *very* wild on that much money, but you can spend a year in Germany — learn the language — go to the opera — take walking trips in the Tyrol — in Switzerland; see England, Scotland, Ireland, France, Belgium, Denmark — you can do a lot in two years.'

He stared at her fascinated.

'Why not? Why not be your own man for once in your life — do what *you* want to — not what other people want you to?'

He murmured something as to 'duty' — but she took him up sharply.

'If ever a man on earth has done his duty, Arthur Peebles, you have. You've taken care of your mother while she was perfectly able to take care of herself; of your sisters, long after they were; and of a wholly able-bodied wife. At present she does not need you the least bit in the world.'

'Now that's pretty strong,' he protested. 'Emma'd miss me — I know she'd miss me — '

Dr Bascom looked at him affectionately. 'There couldn't a better thing happen to Emma — or to you, for that matter — than to have her miss you, real hard.'

'I know she'd never consent to my going,' he insisted, wistfully.

'That's the advantage of my interference,' she replied serenely. 'You surely have a right to choose your doctor, and your doctor is seriously concerned about your health and orders foreign travel — rest — change — and music.'

'But Emma — '

'Now, Arthur Peebles, forget Emma for a while — I'll take care of her. And look here — let me tell you another thing — a change like this will do her good.'

He stared at her, puzzled.

'I mean it. Having you away will give her a chance to stand up. Your letters — about those places — will interest her. She may want to go, sometime. Try it.'

He wavered at this. Those who too patiently serve as props sometimes underrate the possibilities of the vine.

'Don't discuss it with her — that will make endless trouble. Fix up the papers for my taking over the store — I'll draw you a check, and you get the next boat for England, and make your plans from there. Here's a banking address that will take care of your letters and checks — '

The thing was done! Done before Emma had time to protest. Done, and she left gasping to upbraid her sister.

Joan was kind, patient, firm as adamant.

'But how it *looks*, Joan — what will people think of me! To be left deserted — like this!'

'People will think according to what we tell them and to how you behave, Emma Peebles. If you simply say that Arthur was far from well and I advised him to take a foreign trip — and if you forget yourself for once, and show a little natural feeling for him — you'll find no trouble at all.'

For her own sake the selfish woman, made more so by her husband's unselfishness, accepted the position. Yes — Arthur had gone abroad for his health — Dr Bascom was much worried about him — chance of a complete breakdown, she said. Wasn't it pretty sudden? Yes — the doctor hurried him off. He was in England — going to take a walking trip — she did not know when he'd be back. The store? He'd sold it.

Dr Bascom engaged a competent manager who ran that store successfully, more so than had the unenterprising Mr Peebles. She made it a good paying business, which he ultimately bought back and found no longer a burden.

But Emma was the principal charge. With talk, with books, with Arthur's letters followed carefully on maps, with trips to see the girls, trips in which travelling lost its terrors, with the care of the house, and the boarder or two they took 'for company,' she so ploughed and harrowed that long fallow field of Emma's mind that at last it began to show signs of fruitfulness.

Arthur went away leaving a stout, dull woman who clung to him as if he was a necessary vehicle or beast of burden — and thought scarcely more of his constant service.

He returned younger, stronger, thinner, an alert vigorous man, with a mind enlarged, refreshed, and stimulated. He had found himself.

And he found her, also, most agreeably changed; having developed not merely tentacles, but feet of her own to stand on.

When next the thirst for travel seized him she thought she'd go too, and proved unexpectedly pleasant as a companion.

But neither of them could ever wring from Dr Bascom any definite diagnosis of Mr Peebles' threatening disease. 'A dangerous enlargement of the heart' was all she would commit herself to, and when he denied any such trouble now, she gravely wagged her head and said 'it had responded to treatment.'

The Rocking-Chair

A waving spot of sunshine, a signal light that caught the eye at once in a waste of commonplace houses, and all the dreary dimness of a narrow city street.

Across some low roof that made a gap in the wall of masonry, shot a level, brilliant beam of the just-setting sun, touching the golden head of a girl in an open window.

She sat in a high-backed rocking-chair with brass mountings that glittered as it swung, rocking slowly back and forth, never lifting her head, but fairly lighting up the street with the glory of her sunlit hair.

We two stopped and stared, and, so staring, caught sight of a small sign in a lower window — 'Furnished Lodgings.' With a common impulse we crossed the street and knocked at the dingy front door.

Slow, even footsteps approached from within, and a soft girlish laugh ceased suddenly as the door opened, showing us an old woman, with a dull, expressionless face and faded eyes.

Yes, she had rooms to let. Yes, we could see them. No, there was no service. No, there were no meals. So murmuring monotonously, she led the way up-stairs. It was an ordinary house enough, on a poor sort of street, a house in no way remarkable or unlike its fellows.

She showed us two rooms, connected, neither better nor worse than most of their class, rooms without a striking feature about them, unless it was the great brass-bound chair we found still rocking gently by the window.

But the gold-haired girl was nowhere to be seen.

I fancied I heard the light rustle of girlish robes in the inner chamber — a breath of that low laugh — but the door leading to this apartment was locked, and when I asked the woman if we could see the other rooms she said she had no other rooms to let.

A few words aside with Hal, and we decided to take these two, and move in at once. There was no reason we should not. We were looking for lodgings when that swinging sunbeam caught our eyes, and the accommodations were fully as good as we could pay for. So we closed our bargain on the spot, returned to our deserted boarding-house for a few belongings, and were settled anew that night.

Hal and I were young newspaper men, 'penny-a-liners,' part of that struggling crowd of aspirants who are to literature what squires and pages were to knighthood in olden days.

We were winning our spurs. So far it was slow work, unpleasant and ill-paid — so was squireship and pagehood, I am sure; menial service and laborious polishing of armor; long running afoot while the master rode. But the squire could at least honor his lord and leader, while we, alas! had small honor for those above us in our profession, with but too good reason. We, of course, should do far nobler things when these same spurs were won!

Now it may have been mere literary instinct — the grasping at 'material' of the pot-boiling writers of the day, and it may have been another kind of instinct — the unacknowledged attraction of the fair unknown; but, whatever the reason, the place had drawn us both, and here we were.

Unbroken friendship begun in babyhood held us two together, all the more closely because Hal was a merry, prosaic, clear-headed fellow, and I sensitive and romantic.

The fearless frankness of family life we shared, but held the right to unapproachable reserves, and so kept love unstrained.

We examined our new quarters with interest. The front room, Hal's, was rather big and bare. The back room, mine, rather small and bare.

He preferred that room, I am convinced,

because of the window and the chair. I preferred the other, because of the locked door. We neither of us mentioned these prejudices.

'Are you sure you would not rather have this room?' asked Hal, conscious, perhaps, of an ulterior motive in his choice.

'No, indeed,' said I, with a similar reservation; 'you only have the street and I have a real 'view' from my window. The only thing I begrudge you is the chair!'

'You may come and rock therein at any hour of the day or night,' said he magnanimously. 'It is tremendously comfortable, for all its black looks.'

It was a comfortable chair, a very comfortable chair, and we both used it a great deal. A very high-backed chair, curving a little forward at the top, with heavy square corners. These corners, the ends of the rockers, the great sharp knobs that tipped the arms, and every other point and angle were mounted in brass.

'Might be used for a battering-ram!' said Hal.

He sat smoking in it, rocking slowly and complacently by the window, while I lounged on the foot of the bed, and watched a pale young moon sink slowly over the western housetops.

It went out of sight at last, and the room grew darker and darker till I could only see Hal's handsome head and the curving chair-back move slowly to and fro against the dim sky.

'What brought us here so suddenly, Maurice?' he asked, out of the dark.

'Three reasons,' I answered. 'Our need of lodgings, the suitability of these, and a beautiful head.'

'Correct,' said he. 'Anything else?'

'Nothing you would admit the existence of, my sternly logical friend. But I am conscious of a certain compulsion, or at least attraction, in the case, which does not seem wholly accounted for, even by golden hair.'

'For once I will agree with you,' said Hal. 'I feel the same way myself, and I am not impressionable.'

We were silent for a little. I may have closed my eyes, — it may have been longer than I thought, but it did not seem another moment when something brushed softly against my arm, and Hal in his great chair was rocking beside me.

'Excuse me,' said he, seeing me start. 'This chair evidently 'walks,' I've seen 'em before.'

So had I, on carpets, but there was no carpet here, and I thought I was awake.

He pulled the heavy thing back to the window again, and we went to bed.

Our door was open, and we could talk back and forth, but presently I dropped off and slept heavily until morning. But I must have dreamed most vividly, for he accused me of rocking in his chair half the night; said he could see my outline clearly against the starlight.

'No,' said I, 'you dreamed it. You've got rocking-chair on the brain.'

'Dream it is, then,' he answered cheerily. 'Better a nightmare than a contradiction; a vampire than a quarrel! Come on, let's go to breakfast!'

We wondered greatly as the days went by that we saw nothing of our golden-haired charmer. But we wondered in silence, and neither mentioned it to the other.

Sometimes I heard her light movements in the room next mine, or the soft laugh somewhere in the house; but the mother's slow, even steps were more frequent, and even she was not often visible.

All either of us saw of the girl, to my knowledge, was from the street, for she still availed herself of our chair by the window. This we disapproved of, on principle, the more so as we left the doors locked, and her presence proved the possession of another key. No; there was the door in my room! But I did not mention the idea. Under the circumstances, however, we made no complaint, and used to rush stealthily and swiftly up-stairs, hoping to surprise her. But we never succeeded. Only the chair was often found still rocking, and sometimes I fancied a faint sweet odor lingering about, an odor strangely saddening and suggestive. But one day when I thought Hal was there I rushed in unceremoniously and caught her. It was but a glimpse — a swift, light, noiseless sweep — she vanished into my own room. Following her with apologies for such a sudden entrance, I was too late. The envious door was locked again.

Our landlady's fair daughter was evidently shy enough when brought to bay, but strangely willing to take liberties in our absence.

Still, I had seen her, and for that sight would have forgiven much. Hers was a strange beauty, infinitely attractive yet infinitely perplexing. I marveled in secret, and longed with painful eagerness for another meeting; but I said nothing to Hal of my surprising her — it did not seem fair to the girl! She might have some good reason for going there; perhaps I could meet her again.

So I took to coming home early, on one excuse or another, and inventing all manner of errands to get to the room when Hal was not in.

But it was not until after numberless surprises on that point, finding him there when I supposed him downtown, and noticing something a little forced in his needless explanations, that I began to wonder if he might not be on the same quest.

Soon I was sure of it. I reached the corner of the street one evening just at sunset, and — yes, there was the rhythmic swing of that bright head in the dark frame of the open window. There also was Hal in the street below. She looked out, she smiled. He let himself in and went up-stairs.

I quickened my pace. I was in time to see the movement stop, the fair head turn, and Hal standing beyond her in the shadow.

I passed the door, passed the street, walked an hour — two hours — got a late supper somewhere, and came back about bedtime with a sharp and bitter feeling in my heart that I strove in vain to reason down. Why he had not as good a right to meet her as I it were hard to say, and yet I was strangely angry with him.

When I returned the lamplight shone behind the white curtain, and the shadow of the great chair stood motionless against it. Another shadow crossed — Hal — smoking. I went up.

He greeted me effusively and asked why I was so late. Where I got supper. Was unnaturally cheerful. There was a sudden dreadful sense of concealment between us. But he told nothing and I asked nothing, and we went silently to bed.

I blamed him for saying no word about our fair mystery, and yet I had said none concerning my own meeting. I racked my brain with questions as to how much he had really seen of her; if she had talked to him; what she had told him; how long she had stayed.

I tossed all night and Hal was sleepless too, for I heard him rocking for hours, by the window, by the bed, close to my door. I never knew a rocking-chair to 'walk' as that one did.

Towards morning the steady creak and swing was too much for my nerves or temper.

'For goodness' sake, Hal, do stop that and go to bed!'

'What?' came a sleepy voice.

'Don't fool!' said I, 'I haven't slept a wink to-night for your everlasting rocking. Now do leave off and go to bed.'

'Go to bed! I've been in bed all night and I wish you had! Can't you use the chair without blaming me for it?'

And all the time I *heard* him rock, rock,

rock, over by the hall door!

I rose stealthily and entered the room, meaning to surprise the ill-timed joker and convict him in the act.

Both rooms were full of the dim phosphorescence of reflected moonlight; I knew them even in the dark; and yet I stumbled just inside the door, and fell heavily.

Hal was out of bed in a moment and had struck a light.

'Are you hurt, my dear boy?'

I was hurt, and solely by his fault, for the chair was not where I supposed, but close to my bedroom door, where he must have left it to leap into bed when he heard me coming. So it was in no amiable humor that I refused his offers of assistance and limped back to my own sleepless pillow. I had struck my ankle on one of those brass-tipped rockers, and it pained me severely. I never saw a chair so made to hurt as that one. It was so large and heavy and ill-balanced, and every joint and corner so shod with brass. Hal and I had punished ourselves enough on it before, especially in the dark when we forgot where the thing was standing, but never so severely as this. It was not like Hal to play such tricks, and both heart and ankle ached as I crept into bed again to toss and doze and dream and fitfully start till morning.

Hal was kindness itself, but he would insist that he had been asleep and I rocking all night, till I grew actually angry with him.

'That's carrying a joke too far,' I said at last. 'I don't mind a joke, even when it hurts, but there are limits.'

'Yes, there are!' said he, significantly, and we dropped the subject.

Several days passed. Hal had repeated meetings with the gold-haired damsel; this I saw from the street; but save for these bitter glimpses I waited vainly.

It was hard to bear, harder almost than the growing estrangement between Hal and me, and that cut deeply. I think that at last either one of us would have been glad to go away by himself, but neither was willing to leave the other to the room, the chair, the beautiful unknown.

Coming home one morning unexpectedly, I found the dull-faced landlady arranging the rooms, and quite laid myself out to make an impression upon her, to no purpose.

'That is a fine old chair you have there,' said I, as she stood mechanically polishing the brass corners with her apron.

She looked at the darkly glittering thing with almost a flash of pride.

'Yes,' said she, 'a fine chair!'

'Is it old!' I pursued.

'Very old,' she answered briefly.

'But I thought rocking-chairs were a modern American invention!' said I.

She looked at me apathetically.

'It is Spanish,' she said, 'Spanish oak, Spanish leather, Spanish brass, Spanish — .' I did not catch the last word, and she left the room without another.

It was a strange ill-balanced thing, that chair, though so easy and comfortable to sit in. The rockers were long and sharp behind, always lying in wait for the unwary, but cut short in front; and the back was so high and so heavy on top, that what with its weight and the shortness of the front rockers, it tipped forward with an ease and a violence equally astonishing.

This I knew from experience, as it had plunged over upon me during some of our frequent encounters. Hal also was a sufferer, but in spite of our manifold bruises, neither of us would have had the chair removed, for did not she sit in it, evening after evening, and rock there in the golden light of the setting sun.

So, evening after evening, we two fled from our work as early as possible, and hurried home alone, by separate ways, to the dingy street and the glorified window.

I could not endure forever. When Hal came

home first, I, lingering in the street below, could see through our window that lovely head and his in close proximity. When I came first, it was to catch perhaps a quick glance from above — a bewildering smile — no more. She was always gone when I reached the room, and the inner door of my chamber irrevocably locked.

At times I even caught the click of the latch, heard the flutter of loose robes on the other side; and sometimes this daily disappointment, this constant agony of hope deferred, would bring me to my knees by that door, begging her to open to me, crying to her in every term of passionate endearment and persuasion that tortured heart of man could think to use.

Hal had neither word nor look for me now, save those of studied politeness and cold indifference, and how could I behave otherwise to him, so proven to my face a liar?

I saw him from the street one night, in the broad level sunlight, sitting in that chair, with the beautiful head on his shoulder. It was more than I could bear. If he had won, and won so utterly, I would ask but to speak to her once, and say farewell to both for ever. So I heavily climbed the stairs, knocked loudly, and entered at Hal's 'Come in!' only to find him sitting there alone, smoking — yes, smoking in the chair which but a moment since had held her too!

He had but just lit the cigar, a paltry device to blind my eyes.

'Look here, Hal,' said I, 'I can't stand this any longer. May I ask you one thing? Let me see her once, just once, that I may say good-bye, and then neither of you need see me again!'

Hal rose to his feet and looked me straight in the eye. Then he threw that whole cigar out of the window, and walked to within two feet of me.

'Are you crazy,' he said, '*I* ask her! *I!* I have never had speech of her in my life! And *you* — ' He stopped and turned away.

'And I what?' I would have it out now whatever came.

'And you have seen her day after day — talked with her — I need not repeat all that my eyes have seen!'

'You need not, indeed,' said I. 'It would tax even your invention. I have never seen her in this room but once, and then but for a fleeting glimpse — no word. From the street I have seen her often — with you!'

He turned very white and walked from me to the window, then turned again.

'I have never seen her in this room for even such a moment as you own to. From the street I have seen her often — *with you!*'

We looked at each other.

'Do you mean to say,' I inquired slowly, 'that I did not see you just now sitting in that chair, by that window, with her in your arms?'

'Stop!' he cried, throwing out his hand with a fierce gesture. It struck sharply on the corner of the chair-back. He wiped the blood mechanically from the three-cornered cut, looking fixedly at me.

'I saw you,' said I.

'You did not!' said he.

I turned slowly on my heel and went into my room. I could not bear to tell that man, my more than brother, that he lied.

I sat down on my bed with my head on my hands, and presently I heard Hal's door open and shut, his step on the stair, the front door slam behind him. He had gone, I knew not where, and if he went to his death and a word of mine would have stopped him, I would not have said it. I do not know how long I sat there, in the company of hopeless love and jealousy and hate.

Suddenly, out of the silence of the empty room, came the steady swing and creak of the great chair. Perhaps — it must be! I sprang to my feet and noiselessly opened the door. There she sat by the window, looking out, and — yes — she threw a kiss to some one below. Ah, how beautiful she was! How beautiful! I made a step toward her. I held out my hands, I uttered I know not what — when all at once came Hal's quick step upon the stairs.

She heard it, too, and, giving me one look, one subtle, mysterious, triumphant look, slipped past me and into my room just as Hal burst in. He saw her go. He came straight to me and I thought he would have struck me down where I stood.

'Out of my way,' he cried. 'I will speak to her. Is it not enough to see?' — he motioned toward the window with his wounded hand — 'Let me pass!'

'She is not there,' I answered. 'She has gone through into the other room.'

A light laugh sounded close by us, a faint, soft, silver laugh, almost at my elbow.

He flung me from his path, threw open the door, and entered. The room was empty.

'Where have you hidden her?' he demanded. I coldly pointed to the other door.

'So her room opens into yours, does it?' he muttered with a bitter smile. 'No wonder you preferred the 'view'! Perhaps I can open it too?' And he laid his hand upon the latch.

I smiled then, for bitter experience had taught me that it was always locked, locked to all my prayers and entreaties. Let him kneel there as I had! But it opened under his hand! I sprang to his side, and we looked into — a closet, two by four, as bare and shallow as an empty coffin!

He turned to me, as white with rage as I was with terror. I was not thinking of him.

'What have you done with her?' he cried. And then contemptuously — 'That I should stop to question a liar!'

I paid no heed to him, but walked back into the other room, where the great chair rocked by the window.

He followed me, furious with disappointment, and laid his hand upon the swaying back, his strong fingers closing on it till the nails were white.

'Will you leave this place?' said he.

'No,' said I.

'I will live no longer with a liar and a traitor,' said he.

'Then you will have to kill yourself,' said I.

With a muttered oath he sprang upon me, but caught his foot in the long rocker, and fell heavily.

So wild a wave of hate rose in my heart that I could have trampled upon him where he lay — killed him like a dog — but with a mighty effort I turned from him and left the room.

When I returned it was broad day. Early and still, not sunrise yet, but full of hard, clear light on roof and wall and roadway. I stopped on the lower floor to find the landlady and announce my immediate departure. Door after door I knocked at, tried and opened; room after room I entered and searched thoroughly; in all that house, from cellar to garret, was no furnished room but ours, no sign of human occupancy. Dust, dust, and cobwebs everywhere. Nothing else.

With a strange sinking of the heart I came back to our own door.

Surely I heard the landlady's slow, even step inside, and that soft, low laugh. I rushed in.

The room was empty of all life; both rooms utterly empty.

Yes, of all life; for, with the love of a lifetime surging in my heart, I sprang to where Hal lay beneath the window, and found him dead.

Dead, and most horribly dead. Three heavy marks — blows — three deep, three-cornered gashes — I started to my feet — even the chair had gone!

Again the whispered laugh. Out of that house of terror I fled desperately.

From the street I cast one shuddering glance at the fateful window.

The risen sun was gilding all the

housetops, and its level rays, striking the high panes on the building opposite, shone back in a calm glory on the great chair by the window, the sweet face, down-dropped eyes, and swaying golden head.

The Widow's Might

James had come on to the funeral, but his wife had not; she could not leave the children — that is what he said. She said, privately, to him, that she would not go. She never was willing to leave New York except for Europe or for Summer vacations; and a trip to Denver in November — to attend a funeral — was not a possibility to her mind.

Ellen and Adelaide were both there: they felt it a duty — but neither of their husbands had come. Mr Jennings could not leave his classes in Cambridge, and Mr Oswald could not leave his business in Pittsburg — that is what they said.

The last services were over. They had had a cold, melancholy lunch and were all to take the night train home again. Meanwhile the lawyer was coming at four to read the will.

'It is only a formality. There can't be much left,' said James.

'No,' agreed Adelaide, 'I suppose not.'

'A long illness eats up everything,' said Ellen, and sighed. Her husband had come to

Colorado for his lungs years before and was still delicate.

'Well,' said James rather abruptly, 'What are we going to do with Mother?'

'Why, of course — ' Ellen began, 'We *could* take her. It would depend a good deal on how much property there is — I mean, on where she'd want to go. Edward's salary is more than needed now,' Ellen's mental processes seemed a little mixed.

'She can come to me if she prefers, of course,' said Adelaide. 'But I don't think it would be very pleasant for her. Mother never did like Pittsburg.'

James looked from one to the other.

'Let me see — how old is Mother?'

'Oh she's all of fifty,' answered Ellen, 'and much broken, I think. It's been a long strain, you know.' She turned plaintively to her brother. 'I should think you could make her more comfortable than either of us, James — with your big house.'

'I think a woman is always happier living with a son than with a daughter's husband,' said Adelaide. 'I've always thought so.'

'That is often true,' her brother admitted. 'But it depends.' He stopped, and the sisters exchanged glances. They knew upon what it depended.

'Perhaps if she stayed with me, you could

'— help some,' suggested Ellen.

'Of course, of course, I could do that,' he agreed with evident relief. 'She might visit between you — take turns — and I could pay her board. About how much ought it to amount to? We might as well arrange everything now.'

'Things cost awfully in these days,' Ellen said with a crisscross of fine wrinkles on her pale forehead. 'But of course it would be only just *what* it costs. I shouldn't want to *make* anything.'

'It's work and care, Ellen, and you may as well admit it. You need all your strength — with those sickly children and Edward on your hands. When she comes to me, there need be no expense, James, except for clothes. I have room enough and Mr Oswald will never notice the difference in the house bills — but he does hate to pay out money for clothes.'

'Mother must be provided for properly,' her son declared. 'How much ought it to cost — a year — for clothes.'

'You know what your wife's cost,' suggested Adelaide, with a flicker of a smile about her lips.

'Oh, *no*,' said Ellen. 'That's no criterion! Maude is in society, you see. Mother wouldn't *dream* of having so much.'

James looked at her gratefully. 'Board — and clothes — all told; what should you say, Ellen?'

Ellen scrabbled in her small black hand bag for a piece of paper, and found none. James handed her an envelope and a fountain pen.

'Food — just plain food materials — costs all of four dollars a week now — for one person,' said she. 'And heat — and light — and extra service. I should think six a week would be the *least*, James. And for clothes and carfare and small expenses — I should say — well, three hundred dollars!'

'That would make over six hundred a year,' said James slowly. 'How about Oswald sharing that, Adelaide?'

Adelaide flushed. 'I do not think he would be willing, James. Of course if it were absolutely necessary — '

'He has money enough,' said her brother.

'Yes, but he never seems to have any outside of his business — and he has his own parents to carry now. No — I can give her a home, but that's all.'

'You see, you'd have none of the care and trouble, James,' said Ellen. 'We — the girls — are each willing to have her with us, while perhaps Maude wouldn't care to, but if you could just pay the money — '

'Maybe there's some left after all,' suggested Adelaide. 'And this place ought to sell for something.'

'This place' was a piece of rolling land within ten miles of Denver. It had a bit of river bottom, and ran up towards the foothills. From the house the view ran north and south along the precipitous ranks of the 'Big Rockies' to westward. To the east lay the vast stretches of sloping plain.

'There ought to be at least six or eight thousand dollars from it, I should say,' he concluded.

'Speaking of clothes,' Adelaide rather irrelevantly suggested, 'I see Mother didn't get any new black. She's always worn it as long as I can remember.'

'Mother's a long time,' said Ellen. 'I wonder if she wants anything, I'll go up and see.'

'No,' said Adelaide, 'She said she wanted to be let alone — and rest. She said she'd be down by the time Mr Frankland got here.'

'She's bearing it pretty well,' Ellen suggested, after a little silence.

'It's not like a broken heart,' Adelaide explained. 'Of course Father meant well — '

'He was a man who always did his duty,' admitted Ellen. 'But we none of us — loved him — very much.'

'He is dead and buried,' said James. 'We can at least respect his memory.'

'We've hardly seen Mother — under that black veil.' Ellen went on. 'It must have aged her. This long nursing.'

'She had help toward the last — a man nurse,' said Adelaide.

'Yes, but a long illness is an awful strain — and Mother never was good at nursing. She has surely done her duty,' pursued Ellen.

'And now she's entitled to a rest,' said James, rising and walking about the room. 'I wonder how soon we can close up affairs here — and get rid of this place. There might be enough in it to give her almost a living — properly invested.'

Ellen looked out across the dusty stretches of land.

'How I did hate to live here!' she said.

'So did I,' said Adelaide.

'So did I,' said James.

And they all smiled rather grimly.

'We don't any of us seem to be very — affectionate, about Mother,' Adelaide presently admitted, 'I don't know why it is — we never were an affectionate family, I guess.'

'Nobody could be affectionate with Father,' Ellen suggested timidly.

'And Mother — poor Mother! She's had an awful life.'

'Mother has always done her duty,' said James in a determined voice, 'and so did Father, as he saw it. Now we'll do ours.'

'Ah,' exclaimed Ellen, jumping to her feet. 'Here comes the lawyer, I'll call Mother.'

She ran quickly upstairs and tapped at her mother's door.

'Mother, oh Mother,' she cried. 'Mr Frankland's come.'

'I know it,' came back a voice from within. 'Tell him to go ahead and read the will. I know what's in it. I'll be down in a few minutes.'

Ellen went slowly back downstairs with the fine criss-cross of wrinkles showing on her pale forehead again, and delivered her mother's message.

The other two glanced at each other hesitatingly, but Mr Frankland spoke up briskly.

'Quite natural, of course, under the circumstances. Sorry I couldn't get to the funeral. A case on this morning.'

The will was short. The estate was left to be divided among the children in four equal parts, two to the son and one each to the daughters after the mother's legal share had been deducted, if she were still living. In such case they were furthermore directed to provide for their mother while she lived. The estate, as described, consisted of the ranch, the large, rambling house on it, with all the furniture, stock and implements, and some $5,000 in mining stocks.

'That is less than I had supposed,' said James.

'This will was made ten years ago,' Mr Frankland explained. 'I have done business for your father since that time. He kept his faculties to the end, and I think that you will find that the property has appreciated. Mrs McPherson has taken excellent care of the ranch, I understand — and has had some boarders.'

Both the sisters exchanged pained glances.

'There's an end to all that now,' said James.

At this moment, the door opened and a tall black figure, cloaked and veiled, came into the room.

'I'm glad to hear you say that Mr McPherson kept his faculties to the last, Mr Frankland,' said the widow. 'It's true. I didn't come down to hear that old will. It's no good now.'

They all turned in their chairs.

'Is there a later will, madam?' inquired the lawyer.

'Not that I know of. Mr McPherson had no property when he died.'

'No property! My dear lady — four years ago he certainly had some.'

'Yes, but three years and a-half ago he gave

it all to me. Here are the deeds.'

There they were, in very truth — formal and correct, and quite simple and clear — for deeds, James R. McPherson, Sr, had assuredly given to his wife the whole estate.

'You remember that was the panic year,' she continued. 'There was pressure from some of Mr McPherson's creditors; he thought it would be safer so.'

'Why — yes,' remarked Mr Frankland, 'I do remember now his advising with me about it. But I thought the step unnecessary.'

James cleared his throat.

'Well, Mother, this does complicate matters a little. We were hoping that we could settle up all the business this afternoon — with Mr Frankland's help — and take you back with us.'

'We can't be spared any longer, you see, Mother,' said Ellen.

'Can't you deed it back again, Mother,' Adelaide suggested, 'to James, or to — all of us, so we can get away?'

'Why should I?'

'Now, Mother,' Ellen put in persuasively, 'we know how badly you feel, and you are nervous and tired, but I told you this morning when we came, that we expected to take you back with us. You know you've been packing — '

'Yes, I've been packing,' replied the voice behind the veil.

'I dare say it was safer — to have the property in your name — technically,' James admitted, 'but now I think it would be the simplest way for you to make it over to me in a lump, and I will see that Father's wishes are carried out to the letter.'

'Your father is dead,' remarked the voice.

'Yes, Mother, we know — we know how you feel,' Ellen ventured.

'I am alive,' said Mrs McPherson.

'Dear Mother, it's very trying to talk business to you at such a time. We all realize it,' Adelaide explained with a touch of asperity, 'But we told you we couldn't stay as soon as we got here.'

'And the business has to be settled,' James added conclusively.

'It is settled.'

'Perhaps Mr Frankland can make it clear to you,' went on James with forced patience.

'I do not doubt that your mother understands perfectly,' murmured the lawyer. 'I have always found her a woman of remarkable intelligence.'

'Thank you, Mr Frankland. Possibly you may be able to make my children understand that this property — such as it is — is mine now.'

'Why assuredly, assuredly, Mrs McPherson. We all see that. But we assume, as a matter of course, that you will consider Mr McPherson's wishes in regard to the disposition of the estate.'

'I have considered Mr McPherson's wishes for thirty years,' she replied. 'Now, I'll consider mine. I have done my duty since the day I married him. It is eleven hundred days — to-day.' The last with sudden intensity.

'But madam, your children — '

'I have no children, Mr Frankland. I have two daughters and a son. These three grown persons here, grown up, married, having children of their own — or ought to have — were my children. I did my duty by them, and they did their duty by me — and would yet, no doubt.' The tone changed suddenly. 'But they don't have to. I'm tired of duty.'

The little group of listeners looked up, startled.

'You don't know how things have been going on here,' the voice went on. 'I didn't trouble you with my affairs. But I'll tell you now. When your father saw fit to make over the property to me — to save it — and when he knew that he hadn't many years to live, I took hold of things. I had to have a nurse for your father — and a doctor coming: the house was a sort of hospital, so I made it a little more so. I had a half a dozen patients and nurses here — and made money by it. I ran the garden — kept cows — raised my own chickens — worked out doors — slept out of doors. I'm a stronger woman to-day than I ever was in my life!'

She stood up, tall, strong and straight, and drew a deep breath.

'Your father's property amounted to about $8,000 when he died,' she continued. 'That would be $4,000 to James and $2,000 to each of the girls. That I'm willing to give you now — each of you — in your own name. But if my daughters will take my advice, they'd better let me send them the yearly income — in cash — to spend as they like. It is good for a woman to have some money of her own.'

'I think you are right, Mother,' said Adelaide.

'Yes indeed,' murmured Ellen.

'Don't you need it yourself, Mother?' asked James, with a sudden feeling of tenderness for the stiff figure in black.

'No, James, I shall keep the ranch, you see. I have good reliable help. I've made $2,000 a year — clear — off it so far, and now I've rented it for that to a doctor friend of mine — woman doctor.'

'I think you have done remarkably well,

Mrs McPherson — wonderfully well,' said Mr Frankland.

'And you'll have an income of $2,000 a year,' said Adelaide incredulously.

'You'll come and live with me, won't you,' ventured Ellen.

'Thank you, my dear, I will not.'

'You're more than welcome in my big house,' said Adelaide.

'No thank you, my dear.'

'I don't doubt Maude will be glad to have you,' James rather hesitatingly offered.

'I do. I doubt it very much. No thank you, my dear.'

'But what *are* you going to do?'

Ellen seemed genuinely concerned.

'I'm going to do what I never did before. I'm going to *live!*'

With a firm swift step, the tall figure moved to the windows and pulled up the lowered shades. The brilliant Colorado sunshine poured into the room. She threw off the long black veil.

'That's borrowed,' she said. 'I didn't want to hurt your feelings at the funeral.'

She unbuttoned the long black cloak and dropped it at her feet, standing there in the full sunlight, a little flushed and smiling, dressed in a well-made traveling suit of dull mixed colors.

'If you want to know my plans, I'll tell you. I've got $6,000 of my own. I earned it in three years — off my little rancho-sanitarium. One thousand I have put in the savings bank — to bring me back from anywhere on earth, and to put me in an old lady's home if it is necessary. Here is an agreement with a cremation company. They'll import me, if necessary, and have me duly — expurgated — or they don't get the money. But I've got $5,000 to play with, and I'm going to play.'

Her daughters looked shocked.

'Why Mother — '

'At your age — '

James drew down his upper lip and looked like his father.

'I knew you wouldn't any of you understand,' she continued more quietly. 'But it doesn't matter any more. Thirty years I've given you — and your father. Now I'll have thirty years of my own.'

'Are you — are you sure you're — well, Mother,' Ellen urged with real anxiety.

Her mother laughed outright.

'Well, really well, never was better, have been doing business up to to-day — good medical testimony that. No question of my sanity, my dears! I want you to grasp the fact that your mother is a Real Person with some interests of her own and half a lifetime yet.

The first twenty didn't count for much — I was growing up and couldn't help myself. The last thirty have been — hard. James perhaps realizes that more than you girls, but you all know it. Now, I'm free.'

'Where *do* you mean to go, Mother?' James asked.

She looked around the little circle with a serene air of decision and replied.

'To New Zealand. I've always wanted to go there,' she pursued. 'Now I'm going. And to Australia — and Tasmania — and Madagascar — and Tierra del Fuego. I shall be gone some time.'

★   ★   ★

They separated that night — three going East, one West.

The Jumping-Off Place

Two new guests were expected at The Jumping-off Place that night. The establishment was really too full already of Professors, Professorins and — shall we take a lingual liberty and say Professorinii?

The extra ones however had special claims in the mind of Miss Shortridge; claims well weighed by her when she answered their letters.

The Reverend Joseph Whitcomb had been one of her oldest and most honored friends; her minister for some thirty years. She could remember as if of yesterday the hot still Sunday in late May when he was installed in the white wooden church; the warm approval of the entire congregation, with the possible exception of the two oldest deacons and Miss Makepeace — whose name belied her; the instant and continuous adoration of the women, young and old; their artless efforts to attract his attention, win his favor — she herself among the eagerest, worshipping devoutly and afar; — and the chill that fell upon them all when after a few years of this idolatry he brought home a wife after his vacation absence.

A higher call, with a higher salary attached, had taken him to the big city afterward, and in later days she had sat under him there, still worshipping, though with a chastened adoration. It was nine years since she had left that city: —

He had heard of the excellence of her accommodation, his letter read; the quiet intellectual atmosphere of the place — could she be his old parishioner, Miss Shortridge, of Brooktown? And could she put him up for a week or so?

Then she had asked one of the young unmarried Professors if he would mind having his bill reduced three dollars, and sleeping in the woodshed chamber, for a week; and by a comfortable coincidence of desires he was very glad to.

The other letter she was slower in answering.

'Can it be possible that you are the Jean Shortridge I used to know in Brooktown?' this ran. 'Perhaps you won't remember me — Bessie Moore that was — then Mrs Paul Olcott — now Mrs Weatherby. I'm not at all strong, and I've heard of your place as being so refined and quiet, with really excellent food and beds, and very reasonable prices. Could you give me a nice room for two weeks or a month — a large comfortable room, near a bathroom, corner room if possible, and not too many stairs — and what would you charge an old friend?'

There was just one such room unrented, and that was Miss Shortridge's own. With a fortitude rare among those who give board and lodging, she always retained for herself a restful, convenient, quiet room; and enjoyed it.

She read Mrs Weatherby's letter over more than once, her amused smile growing as she studied it.

'I believe I will,' she said to herself at length, 'just for the fun of it. I can manage to dress in the garret for a little while. It won't affect my sleeping, anyhow.'

So she wrote to both that for a week's time she would gladly accommodate them, and found continuing entertainment in the days before their coming in memories and speculations.

'You're not really going to give up your room at last,' protestingly inquired Mrs Professor Joran, who had tried vainly to secure it for a friend.

'Only for a week,' Miss Shortridge explained, 'and under rather exceptional circumstances: The lady coming was a — I have known her since early girlhood.'

The advent of Dr Whitcomb excited more

discussion, and was hailed with a better grace, as no one begrudged the young unmarried Professor's room, while many had desired Miss Shortridge's. They were all extremely polite to their entertainer, however, she not being, so to speak, a professional; taking only a few during the summer months to accommodate; and accommodating beyond the dreams of local competitors.

No professional comments reached her ears regarding the expected arrivals, but she in her own mind, dwelt upon them with growing interest. She remembered Bessie Moore with sharp, almost painful clearness, from the day she was 'teacher's pet' in school, up through her pink and ringleted girlhood, to the white delicacy of her beauty as a bride.

Miss Shortridge had seen her twice as a bride — and as long as she lived would remember those occasions. She could see her still, at nineteen, standing, there in soft veiled whiteness, her small face, pink as a rose beneath the tulle, beside Paul Olcott with his slim young dignity and serious, intellectual face; while she, plain Jean Shortridge, sat, watching, with a pain in her heart that she had honestly believed would kill her.

Not dying, she had gone away to work; and twelve years later found her comfortably established in the office of Horace Weatherby;

his trusted, valued and fairly well-paid secretary.

Slowly, and not unnaturally, through long association she had grown to think more and more of this rather burly and florid gentleman, a successful man, cold and peremptory with subordinates, yet always distinctly courteous to a woman of any class.

As a married man her thoughts of him had been but distantly admiring; when she knew him a widower she had allowed herself to sympathize, afar; when he grew more gracious and approachable with the passing of time, why then — 'What an uncommon old fool I must have been!' said Miss Shortridge to herself, as she summoned those days before her.

Yet she was not old then, only thirty-five, and if a fool, by no means an uncommon one. She had lived in a fool's paradise for a while, it is true, building castles in Spain out of the veriest sticks and straws of friendliness. And then one day, in a burst of exceptionable cordiality, he had invited her to his wedding. And she had gone, veiled, shrinking behind a pillar, scarce able to force herself there, yet wholly unable to stay away.

There was the big, impressive church, her church too, though she hardly knew it with these accessories of carpets, canopies, carriages, crowds; its heaped flowers and triumphant bursts of music. And then, up the aisle, pinker and plumper than ever, in tightly gleaming pearl gray satin, with pearls and lace and a profusion of orange blossoms — Bessie Moore again!

And that was more than twenty years ago!

As the slow train struggled on from little town to little town, its crushed commuters scattering like popped corn at every station, Mrs Horace Weatherby speculated more and more as to the impressive clerical figure a few seats in front of her. The broad square shoulders, the thick gray hair with a wave that was almost a curl — surely she had seen them somewhere.

Sudden need for a glass of water took her down the aisle beyond him, and a returning view brought recognition.

'Dr Whitcomb! — Oh this *is* a pleasure! Do you remember an old parishioner?'

The reverend gentleman rose to the occasion with that marked deference and suave address which had always distinguished his manner to ladies. Remember her! He did indeed. Had he not twice had the privilege of marrying her — with its invaluable perquisite!

Mrs Weatherby could still blush at fifty-three, and did so, prettily.

'It's a great pleasure to meet you, I'm sure,'

she said; and then in a burst of intuition — 'perhaps you're going to Jean Shortridge's too!'

He complimented her on her marvelous perception — 'I am indeed! And you also? — What a pleasure!'

'I've heard such nice things of her place,' said the lady. 'Some friends of mine knew a Professor's family from Lincoln, Nebraska, that went there — they said it was ideal!'

'We are very fortunate, I am sure,' agreed Dr Whitcomb, 'though our stay is but a short one.'

'If I like it I shall stay,' the lady asserted, smiling. 'She'd never turn out an old friend.'

'You have known her a long time?' he inquired.

'O mercy, yes! Since we were babies. She was such a plain little thing — poor dear! — with her hair combed straight back, and a skimpy little pigtail. Grew up plain, too — as you may remember! She had a Sunday school class, you know, in your church. She was a good girl, and clever in a way; clever at books; but not at all brilliant. I think — I don't know as it's any harm to say it after all these years — but I *think* she was very much in love with my first husband — before he married me, of course.'

Dr Whitcomb looked gravely interested,

and made appropriate murmurs as occasion allowed.

'She went to the city to work after that,' continued the lady in continuous flow, 'and the next I heard of her — years later — she was secretary to Mr Weatherby — or had been. That was before I married him. And then — when did I hear of her next? O, yes. My sister met her somewhere about ten years ago. She must have been all of fifty then! — How time does fly!'

'The lady must be much older than you, I am sure,' said Dr Whitcomb.

'Yes, she is; quite a little; but I'm old enough!' She smiled archly.

'Exactly old enough — and not a bit more,' he promptly agreed.

'Luly said she was a perfect wreck!' Mrs Weatherby continued. 'Looked sixty instead of fifty, and so shabby! I don't know what she's done with herself since, I'm sure, but she's somehow got the place at Crosswater (where they have that scientific summer school — fish and things —) and takes boarders in summer — that's all I know.'

'It will be very interesting for you to see her again,' he suggested. 'So many old memories.'

'Some very sad ones, Dr Whitcomb,' murmured the lady, and was easily led or rather was not to be withheld from confiding to his practiced ear the sorrows of her life.

As a recipient of women's griefs Dr Whitcomb was past master; and this assortment was not a novel one. The first husband had proved a consumptive. There were four little children, three little graves, one grown son, always delicate, now haunting the southwest in search of health; with even more of a shadow on his mother's face in speaking of him than his invalidism alone seemed to justify.

Then the husband's early death — her utter loss — her loneliness — did he blame her for marrying again?

Indeed he did not. Marriage was an honorable estate; women especially needed a protecting arm. He trusted that her later happiness had overcome the memory of pain.

But here the appeal to his sympathies was stronger than before.

'O, Dr Whitcomb! You don't know! I can never tell anyone all I've been through! I lived with Mr Weatherby for twenty years — it was a martyrdom, Dr Whitcomb!'

The worthy doctor had a fairly accurate knowledge of his former wealthy parishioner's life and character, and he nodded his head in grave sympathy, the long clean-shaven upper lip pursed solemnly.

'It was not only drink, Dr Whitcomb

— that I could have forgiven! — It is such a relief to speak to you! — Of course I never say a word against him — but you know!'

'I do indeed, Mrs Weatherby. You have my sincerest sympathy. You have suffered much — but suffering often leads us Heavenward!'

Meanwhile the lady did not forget a truth long known to her — that men like sympathy as well as women — and presently drew from him the admission that his health was far from good, asthma admitted, other troubles merely hinted at; and that widower-hood was also lonely.

He did not, however, confide to her the uncertain condition of his financial outlook; his lifelong inability to save; his increasing difficulty in finding a pulpit to satisfy his pride — or even his necessity.

Nor did she, for all her fluent recital, hint at the sad deficiencies revealed when the estate of the late Horace Weatherby came to settlement; which was indeed unnecessary, for he had heard these facts.

The Crosswater stage took them, swaying and joggling in its lean-cushioned seats, through the shadowy afternoon woods and along a sluggish brook that curved through encroaching bushes and spread lazily out in successive ponds, starred with white lilies.

When the road seemed to stop short off and end nowhere, with only blue water and blue sky as alternatives, a short turn round a bunch of cedars brought them to Miss Shortridge's door.

'Why, Jean Shortridge! I'd never have known you in the world!' cried Mrs Weatherby, trying to kiss her affectionately, and somehow missing it as her hostess turned to greet Dr Whitcomb.

'I am delighted to meet you again, Miss Shortridge,' he said, holding her hand impulsively in both his. 'How well you look! How young — if you will pardon me — how young you look!'

Even Mrs Weatherby, jealously scrutinizing her old friend, could not deny that there was something in what he said. Her own bright color and plump outlines had long since given way to the dragging softness of a face well nursed, but little used; expressing only the soft negation of an old child; and her figure now took shape more from the stays without than from the frame within.

Jean Shortridge stood erect and lightly upon her feet. She moved with swift alertness, and carried herself with agility. Her face was healthily weatherbeaten; high colored from sun and wind; her eyes bright and steady.

She was cordial, but not diffuse; installed

them presently in their respective rooms, and sat smiling and well-gowned at the head of her table when they came to supper.

In the days that followed the new guests learned from the old ones much of their hostess's present and recent achievements. This was her third season here, it appeared, and she was regarded as a wonder; she had bought this old place — mortgaged — and was understood to be paying the mortgage, or to have paid it; she was liked and respected in the little community and considered a solid citizen in spite of her wild eccentricity — she slept out of doors!

All this was commonly known, but what Mrs Weatherby wanted to know, and, if the truth must be told, Dr Whitcomb also, was the tale of those years unaccounted for since Jean Shortridge had last been 'sighted' — and set down as an absolute wreck.

It was extremely difficult to get Miss Shortridge's ear. Her bedchamber on the roof of a porch was inaccessible to others, and she sought that skyey chamber immediately after supper. She was a-foot at dawn and at work, really at work, in her garden. Not a rose garden this, but several acres of highly cultivated land, which the active lady 'worked with her hands,' enough to satisfy the most ardent Tolstoyan.

Small time had she for casual conversation save at meals, and then competition was heavy.

So Mrs Weatherby must needs content herself, during a too short week of good air, good sleep, good food, and good company, with a very pretty campaign of 'friendliness' directed against that smoothly defended fortress of Dr Whitcomb's elderly affections.

Well used was the plump widow to these lines of attack; but even better used was he to all the arts of courteous evasion. Not for nothing had he been a popular minister for nearly fifty years.

It was Friday evening (they had arrived on a Saturday) before, at Dr Whitcomb's direct solicitation, Miss Shortridge agreed to give him an hour, Mrs Weatherby promptly chipping in to urge 'her room' as an excellent place for a talk.

It was; and Miss Shortridge in her own favorite chair looked more than ever the hostess; cordial, friendly, quite at ease.

'Now, Jean Shortridge!' Mrs Weatherby began, 'we are old friends, and you needn't make any mystery with us. We want to know what you *did* — what on earth you did — to — well — to *arrive* like this!'

'Is this what you call 'arriving'?' asked Miss Shortridge. 'I'm simply a hard-working woman with her living to earn — and earning it!'

'And a benefactor to society in that process!' blandly interposed the clergyman.

'So is every honest worker, surely!' she suggested, 'but I know what you mean, Mrs Weatherby — I met your sister some seven or eight years ago — and I fancy she gave a pretty bad account of me.'

'A sad account, Jean — not bad. She said you were not looking at all well.'

'No, I was not looking well — nor feeling well — nor doing well,' Miss Shortridge admitted.

'And now you are all three,' said Dr Whitcomb, with an inclination of the head and his admiring smile.

She laughed happily. 'Thank you — I am,' she frankly agreed. 'Well, this is what happened. I was fifty, practically — forty-eight, that is — no money — no health — no happiness.' Here her eyes rested a moment on Mrs Weatherby's soft sagging face. 'You see I never married and all I had earned was spent as it came; for mother for a long time — and doctors. I had no talent in particular, and it was increasingly hard to get work as a stenographer. They want them young and quick and pretty. So — it seemed to me then that I had come to the jumping-off place.'

Her hearers exchanged glances.

'Yes, that's why I named the place — but it's a good name anyhow — and then I got hold of a book — found it by chance in the public library — ' Miss Shortridge paused and heaved a large sigh. 'That *was* a book!' she said.

'What was it?' eagerly inquired Mrs Weatherby.

'It was called 'The Woman of Fifty'; author, one 'A. J. Smith.' But that book was written for *me*! It told me what to do and I did it — and it was all true.'

'What was it? Oh, do tell us! What did you do?' Mrs Weatherby urged.

'I began to live,' said Miss Shortridge. 'You see I thought my life was ended — such as it was — and pitied myself abominably. I got a new notion out of the book — that there was just as much life as ever there was, and it was mine; health — power — success — happiness.'

'And so you 'demonstrated' — is that the phrase?' Dr Whitcomb asked benignly.

'And so I went to work,' she replied.

'Work isn't always easy to get, is it?' inquired Mrs Weatherby.

'Oh, yes — the kind I did. I selected a healthy suburban town — with a good library — and took a kitchen job for five months.

Made my own terms — a good reading lamp and a place to sleep out of doors. I worked hard, slept well, ate good food, and saved money. Every evening I read an hour.'

'May we ask what you read?' asked Dr Whitcomb.

'About nature; about health; about market gardening; and the lives of people who dared to be different. That was a good winter! By June I had over a hundred dollars. All that summer I lived on it. I tramped, rode on trolley cars, lived out of doors — rested. How I rested! Never before in my life had I learned what this world was really like.

'In wet spells I'd board at some farm house. And I gradually settled on the place where I wanted to live the next year — the man was a market gardener — I wanted to learn the business. I worked out doors and in that year; no time to read, slept like a log, grew strong — saved money.

'I got acquainted, too, and learned a lot about horses and pigs and hens, as well as garden stuff. By the end of the second year I had 450 dollars and some experience. Then I went in with a woman who took summer boarders. She rented me her garden, I furnished enough for the house to pay for it; and I could sell what I had left. I made a lot that year.

'Then I heard of this place, got it on good

terms (it was heavily mortgaged you see), and — well, I've paid the mortgage. I own it clear.'

'A magnificent record!' said Dr Whitcomb.

'But how hard you have worked — how hard you work now!' Mrs Weatherby exclaimed. 'I don't see how you stand it.'

'I like it, you see,' said their hostess. 'I like it while I'm doing it, I make a good living by it, and I've got something to look forward to. When I've saved enough I'm going to take a year off, and travel.'

'But — it's not like having a family,' Mrs Weatherby ventured.

'No, it's not. I wish I had a family . . . But since I haven't — why, I might as well have a life of my own. By the time I'm sixty I mean to take that year abroad I speak of. After that I'll keep on earning. Buy me an annuity, perhaps. There is a home for old people in Los Angeles, I've heard, that's pretty near perfect. I might go there to finish up.'

She looked so cheerful, so alert, so capable and assured, and full of hope, so perplexingly young in spite of her gray hair, that Mrs Weatherby was puzzled in her estimate of age.

'Aren't you older than I am, Jean,' she said. 'You used to be.'

Jean laughed. 'Certainly I am. I'm fifty-seven; you're fifty-three. We've both got many years to look forward to.'

'I don't see how you work such financial miracles, Miss Shortridge,' the clergyman protested. 'Surely it is not open to every woman of middle age to achieve independence as easily.'

'Perhaps they wouldn't all find it easy,' she answered. 'It did take some courage, and a definite, sustaining purpose. But the way is wide open. You see I have three lines of work: I raise vegetables and fruits and sell them during the summer. I preserve and can all I do not sell or use, and the boarders during the summer are a great help. By the way, Mrs Weatherby, are you to take the morning stage, or the afternoon?'

'Why, I was hoping you'd let me stay longer,' said that lady lamely; 'I'm very comfortable here; it has done me ever so much good.'

'I am sorry, but I cannot spare the room,' Miss Shortridge replied.

Dr Whitcomb did not wait for her to ask his hour of leaving — 'The morning stage, if you please; and I am extremely grateful for this pleasant visit. It has been a great pleasure, too, to renew our old acquaintance.'

He was up betimes next morning, early enough to find Miss Shortridge in her well kept garden hard at work. He begged a few moments' talk with her, and used his best powers to attract and hold her attention. He spoke of the changes of life; of her long, patient struggle to support herself and care for her mother; of her phenomenal enterprise and success.

She listened gravely, picking her beans with a deft, practiced hand, and stepping slowly along between the dew-wet rows, while he followed.

Then in deeper, softer tones he referred to his own life; to the pain of loss and loneliness; the injury to his work. He longed for true companionship to the end of the journey. Would she, for the time of rich autumnal peace, be his companion?

It is said that all women have at least one offer of marriage; but Jean Shortridge never expected to receive her first at fifty-seven. She thanked him sincerely for the compliment he paid her, but was not inclined to accept it.

He urged her to take time; to think it over. This was no boyish appeal, but a calm proposal for the joining of their declining years; no mad young passion, but real friendship; understanding; a warm, appreciative affection; she must think it over.

He went away on the morning stage, Mrs Weatherby accompanying him, at some inconvenience in the matter of packing.

Miss Shortridge considered her first offer of marriage for a full week, and then declined it.

'Why should I?' she said to herself. 'I always hated nursing. Let Bessie have him, too!'

But Bessie failed this time.

We do hope that you have enjoyed reading this large print book.

Did you know that all of our titles are available for purchase?

We publish a wide range of high quality large print books including:
Romances, Mysteries, Classics
General Fiction
Non Fiction and Westerns

Special interest titles available in large print are:
The Little Oxford Dictionary
Music Book
Song Book
Hymn Book
Service Book

Also available from us courtesy of Oxford University Press:
Young Readers' Dictionary
(large print edition)
Young Readers' Thesaurus
(large print edition)

For further information or a free brochure, please contact us at:
Ulverscroft Large Print Books Ltd.,
The Green, Bradgate Road, Anstey,
Leicester, LE7 7FU, England.
Tel: **(00 44) 0116 236 4325**
Fax: **(00 44) 0116 234 0205**

Other titles published by
The House of Ulverscroft:

SHE

H. Rider Haggard

Horace Holly, a young Cambridge professor, is charged with the task of raising a colleague's son, Leo, after his father's untimely death. Holly is also given a mysterious box, with express instructions not to open it until Leo turns 25. The contents of this box lead the pair, accompanied by a faithful servant, to the east coast of Africa, where they are shipwrecked and forced to make a perilous journey to an uncharted region in the heart of the continent. Ambushed and captured by a savage tribe of natives, they are taken to their leader, a mysterious white queen, who hides a deadly secret . . .

THE RED BADGE OF COURAGE

Stephen Crane

Henry Fleming is an ordinary farm boy turned soldier, with romantic notions about the glory of war. But, as the tedium of his regiment's encampment without action provides ample time for self-reflection, disquieting thoughts begin to prey upon his mind: doubts as to whether, in combat, he will stand his ground valiantly — or flee ignominiously. Then the regiment receives orders to march, and Henry finds himself flung into the maelstrom of battle. Amidst the blood, the acrid smoke, and the unworldly wails of the dying, his courage will be put to the ultimate test . . .

GULLIVER'S TRAVELS

Jonathan Swift

Lemuel Gulliver, surgeon to the *Antelope*, sets sail for the South Seas. But the craft is shipwrecked and he is washed up, barely concious, on the coast of Lilliput. Gulliver wakes to find himself tethered to the ground and surrounded by a multitude of people, all of six inches tall . . . However, Gulliver's adventures do not end there. Future voyages will see him cast up on various strange shores, and endeavouring to navigate the intricacies of increasingly bizarre societies — those of the giants of Brobdingnag, abstracted scientists of Laputa, philosophical Houyhnhnms, and terrifying, brutish Yahoos . . .